The Ho[illegible] a[illegible] Dra[illegible]on

Trials of Friendship

CW01582104

Written and illustrated by

Marcus Mason-Williams

FUZZY FLAMINGO

First published in 2024 by Fuzzy Flamingo
Copyright © Marcus Mason-Williams 2024

Marcus Mason-Williams has asserted his right to be identified as the author of this Work in accordance with the Copyright, Designs and Patents Act 1988.

ISBN: 978-1-7390943-2-4

All rights reserved.
No part of this publication may be reproduced, stored in a retrieval system, or transmitted in any form or by any means, electronic, mechanical, photocopying, recording or otherwise, without the prior permission of the copyright owner.

Editing and design by Fuzzy Flamingo
www.fuzzyflamingo.co.uk

A catalogue for this book is available from the British Library.

To all neurodiverse people, young and old,
who dream of making their mark,
strive to create a better world
and have a passion for adventure.

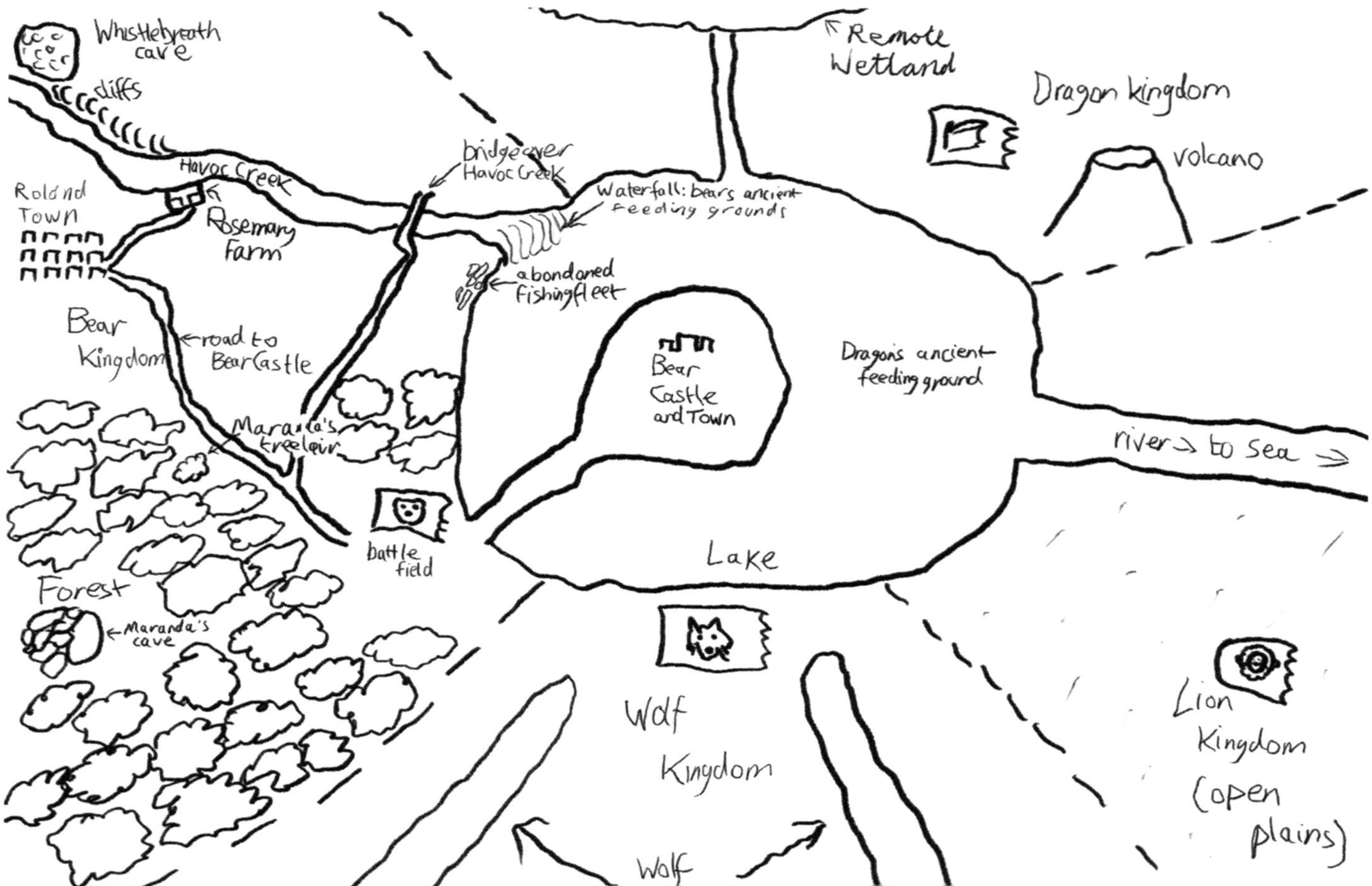

Whistlebreath cave
cliffs
Havoc Creek
Roland Town
Rosemary Farm
bridge over Havoc Creek
Waterfall: bears ancient feeding grounds
Remote Wetland
Dragon kingdom
volcano
abandoned fishing fleet
Bear Kingdom
road to Bear Castle
Bear Castle and Town
Dragon's ancient feeding ground
river → to sea
Maranda's tree lair
battle field
Lake
Forest
Maranda's cave
Wolf Kingdom
Wolf
Lion Kingdom (open plains)

CHAPTER 1

The Journey Begins

Once upon a time, in a land known as Muddle Worth, there were four kingdoms, each named after the animals who roamed their land and were respected by the people. They were the Kingdom of Dragon, the Kingdom of Bear, the Kingdom of Wolf and the Kingdom of Lion. One hundred years ago, these kingdoms split apart, each taking their own stretch of land. The Lion Kingdom was on the vast open plains, the Dragon Kingdom was right next to a steaming volcano, the Wolf Kingdom was situated on a high plateau between two deep canyons. The Bear Kingdom included a large peninsula, stretching into the middle of a vast lake, close to the centre of Muddle Worth. The lake and peninsula had, for centuries, been the place where all the dragons and bears of the land gathered to fish, drink and feed. The men who established the Kingdom of Bear drove the dragons and bears away from their fishing grounds and built their castle on the peninsula. The dragons and bears retreated to another fishing ground in a remote wetland far away from human presence. But in recent years, the wetland fishing grounds began to dry up and the dragons and bears were now growing hungry.

After the split, all the kingdoms lived without any conflict whatsoever. Until, one day, an event took place in the Kingdom of Bear, which threatened the established peace.

The Kingdom of Bear was ruled by a wonderful king and queen along with their twelve-year-old daughter, Princess Maranda, whose great-great-grandfather was the first King of Bear. The princess enjoyed art and nature. She was also autistic. Her parents wanted to prepare her for the duties and responsibilities of ruling the kingdom, but Maranda wanted more out of life. She dreamed of living in harmony with the creatures she loved most in the realm, its dragons!

One spring night on the lake, a group of fishermen was discussing what more they were likely to catch that night. They had already caught a great number of trout, salmon and eel and were about to set off for home, when, all of a sudden, an unexpected creature flew out of nowhere. With its ice breath, it froze the fishing fleet and most of the fishermen and stole their catch. A few of the fishermen survived. They were terrified and rushed back to the castle, desperate to tell the king and queen about what had happened.

After the whole tale was told, the king realised that the only kind of creature in Muddle Worth that could breathe elements was a dragon. He assembled a group of his best knights to go out, find the offending dragon and capture it. Princess Maranda was not so sure that a dragon would attack villagers fishing without a reason, and she hoped that they wouldn't find the dragon. The knights searched until they found the abandoned fishing fleet run aground near the entrance to Havoc Creek. They thought that the creature who had attacked the fleet could not be far away. The creek was in a canyon with tall, sheer cliffs.

Further along the cliffs, the dragon was sheltering in a cave, where she had laid eleven eggs. She had brought the fish back to feed her babies when they hatched. She lay on her eggs to incubate them, knowing that one egg was especially valuable, as, just like one egg in every clutch of whistle-breath dragon eggs, it had magical properties.

Suddenly, the knights appeared at the entrance to her cave. "Spread out," said the knight's leader, "the beast can't be far."

They were hoping for the element of surprise, but the dragon heard them, quickly covered her eggs with leaves and hid.

They all searched, until one of the knights found the place where the eggs were hidden. "Hey!" he called. "I've found some dragon eggs. What shall we do with them?"

The captain gave the order to destroy them, but the mother dragon threw ice shards from her tail, stunning the knights. She did all she could to prevent the men from grabbing her eggs, blowing ice from her mouth and swiping them with her tail. The leader threw some magic powder at the dragon, making her collapse and quickly fall asleep. Since the creature was unconscious, the knights decided to take her in alive. As for the eggs, some were destroyed, others were scattered, but, by chance, the magical egg was knocked right out of the cave, down the slopes of the canyon and finally into Havoc Creek.

When the knights reached the Kingdom of Bear, they showed the dragon to the king, queen and princess. After telling them the story of the capture, the knight's leader asked, "What shall we do with it, Your Majesty?"

The king looked at his wife and daughter and said, "Put the dragon in the dungeon, until we decide which of our most

promising young knights will have the right to fight it as a rite of passage."

When Maranda heard what her father said, she was devastated; she felt overwhelmed by the unexpected, heartbreaking news and needed time to process, before deciding what she could do. She ran to her room in tears, refusing to speak to her parents, especially her father.

The dragon was placed into the dungeon, as the king had commanded. But the queen was worried; she knew that the consequence of killing a dragon could be the Kingdom of Dragon declaring war on the Kingdom of Bear. As for Maranda, she eventually stopped crying, knowing that there was something bigger afoot. She resolved to harness the passion and power to focus, which her autism gave her, to dedicate her life to finding the reason for the dragon's attack on the fishermen and to saving the dragon.

As for the magical egg, it continued floating down the river. To where? We'll see…

CHAPTER 2

The Birth of a Horse

On the opposite banks of Havoc Creek, further downstream, there was a patch of beautiful countryside with a farm called Rosemary Farm, owned by Farmer Samuel Rosemary and his wife, Bonnie. They had a twelve-year-old son named Richard and they kept many animals, including cows, chickens, goats, sheep, pigs, horses, ducks, geese and one donkey named Devon. Farmer Rosemary worked hard on the land, while Bonnie mainly worked inside the house and looked after the farmyard animals. The farmer was a good man and a fair master. Samuel and Bonnie were trying to prepare Richard for a hard-working life as a farmer. Richard loved his life on the farm, but his autism led to him having problems knowing how to make friends; the other kids called him a lowlife farm boy and a toadstool, due to his size, and that upset him deeply.

Fortunately, Richard was about to encounter some situations that would allow him to use his autistic superpowers to achieve great things, stand up for others and change his life for the better. It all started the same spring day the whistle-breath dragon attacked the fishing fleet. One of Farmer Rosemary's pregnant mares, Sophie, started going into labour. That morning, when Richard went into the stable to feed Sophie, he found her lying down, panting hard. He rushed off to tell his parents. "Mum, Pop, you've got to come quick," he cried. "Sophie looks like she's in labour."

"Well, what are we waiting for?" said the farmer. "Let's go and help our sweet mare."

"I'll go and collect some blankets and water," Bonnie said. Both father and son ran to the stables while Bonnie rushed into the kitchen. By the time they arrived, Sophie was shaking her head, tossing her hooves around and whinnying in agony.

The farmer moved into the stable and spoke quietly to her. "Shh, easy, Soph, I'm here, girl, it's all right." He put his right hand on her head to reassure her and calm her down. "It's okay to come in," he said to his family. Then he said, "Honey, I need you to use a blanket on Sophie's head to keep her calm. Richard, I need you to help me deliver the foal."

Bonnie and Richard both nodded and prepared to help. Bonnie knelt by the mare and gently put the blanket over her head, while Richard and Samuel stood by the tail end. The farmer showed Richard how to wash his hands and arm thoroughly. Samuel then stretched his arm into the birth canal, until he could feel a tiny muzzle, then one hoof and then another. He turned to his son. "Okay," he said, "I know it's a bit unpleasant, but right now, I need you to be strong. Just think of us helping a pregnant cow or ewe and you'll be fine."

At first, Richard was unsure, but then he plucked up the courage. "Okay, Dad, I'm ready." With that, both father and son started working together to pull the foal out of the mother.

"How are you doing over there, honey?" the farmer asked his wife.

"Don't you worry about me," she replied. "You boys just try to get the baby out. It's okay, Sophie," she said to the mare, "just take some deep breaths."

"I can feel a hoof, Dad," said Richard.

"Okay, son, on the count of three, we pull, but not too

hard, just nice and easy," said the farmer. Then he carried on, "One, two, three, pull."

After several more pulls, despite Sophie being exhausted and crying in pain, father and son finally delivered the little creature.

"I've got it," cried Richard. The foal was lying on Richard's lap feeling wet from head to tail. It let out a small neigh, enough to rouse Sophie.

The farmer checked over the foal and said, "It's a boy." Bonnie looked on with tears in her eyes. She was always amazed at the miracle of new life on the farm.

"Aww," she said, "he's beautiful and so adorable."

Sophie got to her feet and started to lick the afterbirth off the colt. The foal had two things on his mind; firstly, to get to his feet, and secondly, to stay at his mother's side. He tried hard to stand up, but getting to his feet wasn't easy.

Sophie believed her son could do it, so she said softly, "You can do it, my boy, just one hoof after the other." With that sweet encouragement from her voice, the colt summoned all his strength and stood up shakily on all four hooves. The colt had a chestnut coat, a white blaze down his face, two white stockings (one on the left front leg and one on the back right leg), along with a golden mane and tail. The Rosemary family chuckled with joy.

"He's a fighter," said Samuel.

"He's a beauty," said Bonnie.

"He's a friend," said Richard. He felt an immediate connection with the colt, as he did with so many animals.

At first, the foal was shy to be around the humans, but with his mother offering gentle encouragement, the farmer helped the colt to his mother's teat.

"There you go, fella, enjoy," Samuel said softly.

"I think he needs a name," Richard told his parents.

"You're right," said his father. "I'm thinking Thunder, or Drifter, or..."

"No, they're just not right," said Richard.

"How about Warm, like a blanket?" said Bonnie.

Richard shook his head. "Wait," he said, "I have a great name for him. I shall call him Chester, after his chestnut coat."

"Chester, eh?" the farmer said. "I like it, don't you, my dear?" he asked his wife.

She gave a beautiful smile. "I love it," she said sweetly.

Then Richard went up to Sophie and asked, "Do you like the name, Sophie?" Sophie neighed in agreement.

When the family left the stable, Richard said to his dad, "He's not just any horse, he's my friend, my Chester."

"Well, son," replied the farmer, "seeing as how you helped deliver and name that colt, you can own and train him. But, before we train him, we must first let him grow up."

Father and son agreed that they would train Chester together when he was old enough.

CHAPTER 3

Playing Together

Sophie and Chester were put in a field with other mares and their foals, who were all grazing, playing and rolling around. To begin with, Chester stayed as close to his mum as he possibly could. But then the chestnut colt began to have lots of energy. It was time for him to run. "Hey, Mum, is it okay for me to run around for a bit?" he said excitedly.

Sophie could see that her son was full of spirit. *Oh, my boy,* she thought proudly. "Okay, Chester, my son," she said, "have fun, but don't run too far, stay where I can see you."

"Aren't you coming?" Chester asked.

"I'll be watching from over here. Now go and stretch out those leg muscles." His mother smiled. With a glint of excitement in his eyes, Chester looked straight ahead, pawed the ground with his right front hoof and then took off. He ran and ran all around the field at such breakneck speed that all the other foals soon fell behind.

Richard was watching the herd from the front gate. He had been fascinated with horses since he was a baby, but the one horse he was really fascinated by was Chester. Every time Chester ran around the meadow, Richard was amazed by his speed and stamina.

When the colt stopped running, he glanced in Richard's direction. The two exchanged looks, then Chester trotted over to his mother and snuggled in close to her. Richard opened the gate and walked up to the pair. The other horses were grazing nearby. As the boy came closer, Chester hid behind his mother.

"It's all right, my son," Sophie said softly, "he just wants to be friendly." Chester still backed away, so his mother decided to show him how to be around humans.

"Hi there, girl," said Richard. "I just want to say hello to your foal." When Richard put his hand up, Sophie kindly put her nose into it, to show Chester that it was safe.

The colt was curious about what his mother was doing with Richard. Sophie encouraged Chester to come closer. Richard had a feeling that it could be overwhelming for him and Chester to have eye contact, so he took things slowly, put his hand out, closed his eyes and waited for Chester to move. Gradually, one hoof after another, Chester approached, then gently put his own nose into the boy's hand.

Richard smiled and said, "Hi, boy, my name is Richard

Rosemary and I'm not going to hurt you." Then Chester allowed Richard to stroke his face.

"Richard," called his father, "I need your help with the chickens." As the farmer approached the gate, he chuckled with delight. "Ha, ha, looks like you've made a friend, son," he said. "Now come on, we've got to collect the eggs."

"Okay, Dad, on my way," called Richard, then he turned to Chester. "I've gotta go and help my dad. You have fun while I'm gone," he said.

After Richard had gone, Sophie said to her son, "Well, what do you think?"

"Well," began Chester, "when the boy touched me, I saw right into his eyes; he looks kind, so I like him and I'm pretty sure he likes me too."

Sophie smiled. She was happy to know that her foal was making a friend on the farm. "Our master has looked after us ever since your grandfather first founded this herd," she told him. "You have a fighting spirit, just like your father; his name was Flame and he was a horse of the Kingdom of Wolf. Despite all the hardness of battle against the enemies of Muddle Worth beyond our borders, both your father and his knight master survived. The knight soon became the new King of Bear, and your father was retired to this farm. I was a young mare when I met him, his heart was like pure sunlight and his spirit was never broken." Then she told Chester that Flame was loyal to her and her family and that his coat was like pure silver. "You have your father's spirit when you run. I hope you will grow up to be loving, loyal, strong and caring like he was." She also advised Chester never to pick a fight with anyone and only to use his teeth and hooves to defend himself and others around him.

Richard came to visit Chester every day, after his morning chores. Together they played chase and hide and seek. Chester did most of the hiding.

One morning, Richard lay down with his head resting on his best friend and showed the colt cloud shapes. Being a horse, Chester didn't understand the shapes of clouds yet, but Richard helped along the way. Then Chester caught sight of cloud shapes that would not only give them a good game but would also change the course of their lives. They were the shapes of a princess riding on a dragon. Chester whinnied at Richard and pointed his head in the direction of the clouds.

"Wow," said Richard, looking amazed, "those clouds look like a princess riding a dragon; what do you reckon, pal?"

"Neigh!" said Chester.

Then the pair heard Richard's mother calling, "Richard, come on inside, it's time for lunch."

"Coming, Mum!" Richard called back. "See you later, boy," he said to Chester. The colt looked at Richard closing the gate behind him and then back at the clouds.

I wonder if this is a sign, he said to himself, as he ran around the field.

CHAPTER 4

The Egg

Havoc Creek ran next to the meadow where the Rosemary Farm horses went to drink. After Richard had gone inside, Sophie took Chester down to the creek for a drink. At first, the colt didn't know what to expect because he had never tasted fresh water before.

"It's okay, Chester, I'll be here," his mother said comfortingly. So, for the first time, Chester took a sip of clear, fresh running water. "What do you think?" asked Sophie after Chester's head came up from drinking.

"Different from milk, but fresh all the same, Mum," answered Chester.

"Well, drink as much as you can, there's no hurry," Sophie said.

Just then, Chester caught sight of something glowing in the water, unlike anything he had ever seen. It was something mystical and magical. He couldn't tell if it was a rock or a pebble. "Hey, Mum," he said, "I see something glowing in the water." Sophie just kept on drinking, but, as Chester continued looking at the shape of the object, he realised it was an egg.

Something inside his soul was telling him to help the egg, another was telling him to listen to his mother. In the end, he decided he wasn't going to let the egg drown. So, he dipped his muzzle into the water and gently picked it up in his teeth.

He turned and took the egg to a different part of the meadow to look for a secure place to hide it, until two older colts, named Oak and Skye, barred his way.

"How are ya doing, little buddy?" asked Oak, the black colt.

"Fine, fellas!" said Chester, his mouth full of egg.

"And what have you got there?" asked Skye, the silver-grey colt.

With his mouth still full, Chester decided to put the egg down. "I've just found this egg in the river. I've saved it from drowning and now I'm trying to find a place to nurture it."

Skye just laughed, but Oak, who was more reasonable and wanted to help, said, "You ought to try Jackson, the cockerel, to see if one of his hens can look after it."

"That's a good idea, thanks, Oak." Oak loosened the latch on the gate, then Chester seized the opportunity and galloped through the farmyard, past the barn and the pond where the ducks and geese were swimming, and then past the farmhouse, until he finally found the hen house. The chickens were strutting around their yard, while Jackson the cockerel was watching.

"Hey, Jackson," cried Chester with the egg still in his mouth. "I need your help."

"What can be more important than watching my flock, young one?" asked Jackson with a sigh.

"Will you please look?" Chester insisted.

The cockerel saw the large, blue egg in the foal's mouth. "Stuff my wattles, what is that?" he cried.

"It's an egg of some sort," Chester said, putting it down on the floor. "And I really need someone to look after it for a while." The hens stopped what they were doing and stared at the thing next to Chester.

"Are you out of your mind?" asked Jackson. "Chester, you can't just drag stray eggs out of the creek; besides, it's too big for any of the hens to sit on."

Chester was about to reply when one of the hens, named Willow, stepped in and said, "I'll look after it." Jackson could not believe his eyes or his ears. "Look, Jackson," said Willow, "whether you agree with this or not, I believe it is our job, as mother hens, to look after eggs, no matter what species they are." She then turned to Chester and said, "Young colt, I admire your caring attitude and I see this egg means something to you, so we'll do what we can for it."

Jackson was, at first, against the idea of housing a strange egg, so he decided to put it to a vote. "All right, all those in favour of keeping the egg, raise your wings," he said. All of the hens lifted up their wings. "All those who oppose?" asked Jackson, but no one did.

So, it was settled. The hens would look after the strange egg until it hatched.

"Thank you, guys, I gotta go," Chester said as he took off and hurried back to the field.

After Chester had galloped away, Willow began pushing the egg right inside the hen house. She shoved it into her own nest.

"You don't think this could be a turkey's egg, do you, dear?" asked a fellow hen.

"I don't know, Rosie," said Willow, "but I will love it with my whole heart." Willow was alert for the presence of the farmer, just like all the hens, because he collected their eggs every day for market and Willow didn't want him to find this special egg.

As soon as Chester arrived back in the field, he found his mother waiting. "What were you doing outside the field?" she asked, concerned for his safety.

"I found an egg in the river; I couldn't just leave it to die," said Chester. "So, I lifted it out of the river and took it all the way to the hen house."

"What type of egg is it?" Sophie asked.

"I don't know," said Chester. "A hen called Willow agreed to raise it as her own, so I hope I saved it in time."

Despite the fact that he had run into the farmyard without telling her, Sophie calmed herself. She was very glad and proud that her son had helped another creature. "Chester," she said, "you have a special gift for helping and bonding with others. We all have our differences and life isn't always easy, so cherish your rare and special bond of friendship with Richard and protect him with your life."

That night, inside the farmhouse, Farmer Rosemary was settling down to dinner with his wife and son.

"Richard, how was your day?" asked his mother.

"It was amazing. I spent the morning with my friend, Chester," he said. "I tell you, Mum, Chester is just what you'd expect a friend to be like. Sure, he was shy at first, but the longer I've been with him, the more I see his personality."

“Look, son,” said his father, “the young colt may be good, but you have to make sure that people can be your friends too.”

“Your father is right,” added Bonnie, “it’s time you gave people a chance; they’re not so bad, once you get to know them.”

But Richard didn’t take it so well. “Why? What have people ever done for me but give me a hard time? Especially other kids. All they ever do is push me around and mock me because of my size and because they don’t understand that autism just gives me different strengths and not weakness.”

Emotions had got the better of Richard, so he ran upstairs to his room, leaving his parents to figure out how they could help their son to make friends with other children.

CHAPTER 5

The Dragon's Arrival

After the Rosemary family went to sleep and all the chickens were roosting inside the hen house, the strange, magical egg started to crack. A foot with talons burst out, then another; next came one rear leg and then another. Soon a tail came through. All the chickens were awoken by the hatching. The creature started rolling around until finally it could feel all four feet on the floor.

"What's going on?" said one hen.

"I don't know," answered another.

Finally, the egg exploded into hundreds of pieces, wings appeared and the strange creature emerged. Willow went over to where it was lying in the middle of the coop, amongst a gathering of hens. She gently nudged the little creature and then said softly, "Are you all right?"

It slowly opened its eyes and looked up at her. Then it spoke. "Mama!" it said. The chickens had never seen such a strange and unusual creature; its skin was covered in scales instead of feathers, and it had talons on all four feet.

"It's a boy!" Willow said to the flock. The chickens didn't yet know it was a dragon. All they saw was a creature unlike any they had ever seen before.

Jackson, the cockerel, woke up and strutted over to see what was going on. When he saw the baby dragon, he was

shocked. "Willow, get away from that thing," he protested, pushing her away.

"No, no, no, Jackson," said Willow, "he isn't harming anyone; what has got into you?"

"That thing is not a chicken; it cannot be one of us," he said firmly. As soon as the dragon got to its feet, Jackson turned on it. But Willow blocked his way, standing firmly. The other hens looked surprised to see Willow standing up to their cockerel. They both stared at each other, until Jackson realised that this was one contest he couldn't win. He took a deep breath and composed himself. "Do we know where its real family is?" he asked.

"First of all, 'it' is a 'he' and, when Chester brought him to us, he said nothing about his real family being in sight," Willow said.

"Are you sure?" Jackson asked again.

"Yes, there was no one else where he found the egg," she answered.

The cockerel looked at his flock, then at Willow, and finally said, "Then you may keep him."

Willow smiled and hugged Jackson. "Oh, Jackson, I am so

relieved, and I know he'll be a good son," she said.

"Just because he can stay, doesn't make him my own son," Jackson said. He then turned to the flock. "Let's all get some sleep tonight," he ordered.

With that, the chickens went back to their nests and Willow was left with her new child. When she looked into his eyes, she noticed that there was something wise, noble and intelligent about him.

"What are you going to call him, dearie?" Rosie asked before she went to bed.

"I think I shall call him Wisdom," Willow said, smiling.

"Wow, that's wonderful, dear," said Rosie. "Well, I must get back to my own eggs now. Good night, dear."

As soon as all the chickens went to bed, Willow tucked Wisdom in, and they all settled down to sleep.

The next morning, Chester and his mum were out in the field with the rest of the herd, grazing. On the other side of the farm, in the chicken coop, Wisdom was playing hide and seek with the other newly hatched chicks. "Eight, nine, ten; ready or not, here come the talons," he called. To begin with, the chicks were terrified of the strange creature. But, over time, as spring changed to summer, they grew quite accustomed to Wisdom; even a young cockerel called Tonto, who'd hatched the same day. In fact, the young dragon and young cockerel were just like brothers. Soon, they started playing games of chase.

"You'll never catch me, scaly boy!" Tonto teased.

"Oh, I wouldn't be so sure, brother," said Wisdom.

Jackson was watching over the flock and looking out for the farmer and the boy, but he couldn't help scowling at Wisdom. *I've got my eye on you, scales,* he thought. Suddenly, he heard Farmer Rosemary coming with Richard. "Farmer's coming," he called.

Willow didn't want the farmer to discover her adopted son because, if he was found, he could be kicked out of the farm or killed. So, she called to him, "Wisdom, you must hide yourself."

Some kids wouldn't obey their parents, but Wisdom realised from his mother's tone that she meant it, so he hid right at the back of the nest boxes.

"Now, son, let's get those eggs," said the farmer. As soon as they were inside the hen house, they started collecting the eggs that had not hatched.

"How many do we need, Dad?" asked Richard.

His father answered, "As many as we can, my boy." But while they were collecting eggs, they failed to realise that there was a strange creature crawling through the back of the coop.

After they'd collected all the eggs, they set off to milk the cows. As soon as the farmer and Richard left, Wisdom revealed himself, surprising Willow, who realised that he had changed colour to blend in with the background.

After finishing his chores with his father, Richard came to the field to catch up with his friend. "Hi Chester, I've got an apple for you," he called.

The colt turned to Sophie and asked, "Mother, why does he carry an apple with him?"

"I think you'll find he wants to treat you and be your friend, my boy," she replied. She explained that it's okay to take a treat, but only if the person was good, so Chester galloped over to the fence.

"Hey, you," Richard said. Chester took the apple in his mouth and crunched it, then the boy put his hand on his friend's head. "Do you want to play, bud?" he asked. In no time at all, the two friends were playing chase all around the field. The other horses found the sight of a colt and a human boy playing together odd, but Sophie found the sight pleasing because her son had a friend. The farmer and his wife also found the sight of their son playing with the colt pleasing because they wanted him to be happy, as well as learn about farming, to be prepared for his future.

CHAPTER 6

Horse Meets Dragon

A few days later, Richard and Chester played tag and many other games until they were both so out of breath, they had to stop for a rest.

"I know you can't talk, but that doesn't mean you're not a good listener, pal," said Richard. "So, I'm going to tell you something I haven't told my parents. You see, I wish I was a brave knight, protecting all of Muddle Worth, and I wish you were my partner in life or death." Chester listened and started to pick up what his boy was saying and dreaming. Richard told him that he could picture himself with a sword in one hand and a shield in the other, with him and Chester being brothers-in-arms, protecting and serving the entire land of Muddle Worth. Chester liked the idea of his friend riding on his back into battle, even though he didn't quite understand some of the conversation.

"Come on, Richard," called Mrs Rosemary. "Please help us with the rest of the chores." Richard left and Chester returned to the herd.

On the other side of the farm, Wisdom was getting bored with his way of life, hiding from the farmer and his family when they came to feed the chickens. He minded that he wasn't allowed at the dinner tray, even though dragons don't like seed. He started to feel the urge to explore the farm and to find something better to eat for himself. Suddenly, his sensitive nose picked up the whiff of something fresh coming from far away.

Tonto looked up and saw his brother acting strange. "Hey there, Wis, why are you sniffing?" he asked.

"Just something I haven't smelled before, Tonto," said Wisdom, "and it's coming from that direction."

"Let me see, bro," Tonto said. He stepped forward and took a sniff himself. "What you're smelling is probably fish coming from the river," he said.

Wisdom started to advance towards the fence.

"Wait, Wis, if Mum finds you're missing, she will blame me," Tonto said anxiously, but Wisdom started to feel confident inside, perhaps a little too confident…

"Don't worry, Tonto, I'll find my way back with my sniffer," he said.

"Okay, just don't say I didn't warn you," the young cockerel called.

But Wisdom was too far away to hear. In the field, Chester was grazing with the older colts, unaware of the young dragon strolling through the long grass at the edge of the field straight towards the river. When Wisdom reached it, he could see that there were trout, salmon and eel. He was so hungry, he felt like he just wanted to take a bite. Being young and inexperienced, Wisdom had much to learn! He didn't realise that the trick was to wait for the victim to get close and take it by surprise. He splashed and splashed around, but time after time, he couldn't catch his first fish.

The sound of the dragon's splashing attracted Chester's attention. The colt was curious and trotted over to investigate. He came slowly closer, while Wisdom was still focused on trying to catch his first fish, unaware of Chester's presence. At first, he didn't know what to say, but then the colt's courage returned, and he spoke to the creature. "Er, hello, can I help you?" Chester asked.

"No, thank you, I can do this," Wisdom insisted.

"Okay, well how about I just stand here and watch?" said Chester. He was starting to admire this young creature's persistence and hoped it would pay off. After missing time after time, Wisdom finally caught his first fish. When he turned around, he came face-to-face with the chestnut colt. At first, the two creatures were unsure of how to react to each other, but then they both spoke.

"Hi, my name is…" they said together.

"You go first," Chester said.

"No, you go ahead," Wisdom insisted.

"Okay, my name is Chester and I'm a horse," said Chester.

"I'm Wisdom and I'm a chicken," Wisdom said.

Chester raised his eyebrows when Wisdom told him he was a chicken, even though he didn't know what he was either. "I assume you aren't from around here," Chester said.

The dragon was starting to feel confused. "What are you talking about? I was hatched here on the farm," he said, feeling offended.

"Okay, okay," Chester said, trying to make peace. "I didn't mean to offend you. What I mean to say is, do you like to play?"

Wisdom realised that Chester was trying to befriend him.

"Well, I usually only play with my older brother, Tonto, but I guess I can make an exception for you," he said. They both thought hard about what games they could play together, until Wisdom came up with a game of hide and seek. "I'll count and you hide," Wisdom said to his new friend.

"You got it," Chester replied, then took off as soon as Wisdom started counting.

"… Eight, nine, ten; ready or not, here come the talons!" Wisdom called and off he went. Using his keen sense of smell, Wisdom started to track Chester's scent.

Chester tried to hide in the straw in the barn, but, as he was about to learn, it was not easy fooling a dragon's nose.

"I found you, Chester," Wisdom said when he saw the colt's tail showing.

"Aww, rats," Chester grumbled. "I'll get you on the next go."

"Now, now, pal, there's no need to be a sore loser," teased Wisdom.

Instead of reacting in frustration, Chester reacted by laughing, and so Wisdom started laughing too.

"Hey, hey, I bet you can't run as fast as I can," Chester called to Wisdom.

"Are you challenging me?" the young dragon asked, raising an eyebrow.

"Maybe, would you like to find out? If you've got the stomach for it!" the young colt replied.

Then it was one challenge after another, game after game. First racing, hide and seek, then splashing in the river. Through these hours, Chester and Wisdom started to bond and they were becoming good friends. Finally, they lay exhausted on the grass, looking up at the clouds.

"Hey, I've got to ask, what is so special about the white plushie things up there?" Wisdom asked.

Chester looked at his friend in a puzzled sort of way. "You mean you've never seen clouds before?" he asked back.

"Er, no," replied Wisdom.

"Okay. Richard, my human boy, always told me that, if you look up at them, you get to see the spirits wherever you go. Oh, and they also make you feel like you're skipping around in the sky having fun."

Chester then began telling Wisdom about his life at Rosemary Farm, about his boy and about the games they played. Wisdom in return told Chester about his life with the chickens. Then they heard both Chester's mum and Wisdom's adopted mum calling from different directions.

"Well, I'll see you around. Bye until next time," said Chester.

"Ditto," answered Wisdom, and away they both went.

When Chester reached his mother, she seemed very relaxed. "Hello, my boy, did you have fun today?" she asked.

"Yes!" said Chester. "I made a new friend."

"Oh, really?" Sophie asked. "Does this friend have a name?"

"Yep, his name is Wisdom. He may not be from around here, but, I tell you, we had lots of fun, and boy, am I happy today," Chester chortled, smiling.

"Well, as long as you're happy, son, that's what really matters," Sophie said, her face filling with a smile.

When Wisdom arrived back at the chicken coop, Willow, Tonto and the rest of her clutch were waiting for him. Willow looked rather worried. "Are you trying to scare me to death, young egg?" she asked.

"No, Mum, I think I can explain." Wisdom shuddered as he couldn't face his mother's disappointed looks.

"Come with me," she said sternly. Inside the hen house, the young dragon had to face his mum's telling off.

"I distinctly remember telling you to stay hidden inside these walls. Do you know what would happen to you if the farmer and his family find you? You could be taken away, or worse," she went on.

"But, Mum..." began Wisdom, hoping to give his side of the story, but Willow wouldn't hear any of her son's excuses.

"Don't interrupt me, young man, do you have any idea how many eggs I have lost before?" But when she looked at her son feeling sorry for himself, she took a deep breath and composed herself. "Look, my son," she began, "I don't mean to take away your freedom or stop you having fun. I was just worried and concerned for your safety; for our family's safety. Jackson can only look after our flock for so long. You have to play your part on the farm. The humans are not ready to see you yet, so can you please try to tell me where you are going, before you leave?" She then smiled and put her wing around Wisdom's shoulder. "Tell me your side of the story," she asked gently.

At last, Wisdom was ready to tell Willow what he had been up to. Tonto was outside the door listening. "Well, I smelled something called fish and some kind of urge told me to follow that smell and catch my own lunch. I even met someone. His name is Chester and he's a horse."

"So, you met Sophie's son, that's good. Tell me more when you're ready."

Wisdom told Willow all about his time with Chester and that they were starting to become friends. They talked late into the night.

At the same time, inside their stall, Chester was telling his mother all about Wisdom and about the fun they had together.

"He sounds good fun this Wisdom; I'd like to meet him. I've known Willow a long time, so I'd like to hear the story of her new son," Sophie said.

"Really, so you want to meet my new friend?" Chester asked, feeling really pleased. His mum nodded. "Oh, thank you, Mum, thank you, thank you, you won't regret this!"

CHAPTER 7

Run from Home

At the Kingdom of Bear, the years flew by like leaves blowing off a tree into the wind. At the castle, Princess Maranda had just turned sixteen. She was growing into a young woman and developing deeper learning about nature and conservation and a strong sense of justice. Sadly, her father, King Thomas, still had the female whistle-breath dragon locked in the dungeon, planning to use her as a rite of passage for the next really talented young knight who came to train at Bear Castle. For the four years since the dragon's capture, the king had managed to keep her secret from the kings of the three other Muddle Worth kingdoms. He had sworn all his knights to secrecy and only allowed his most trusted knights and servants access to the dungeons. King Thomas continued to fear that war might break out if the King of Dragon learned about the dragon's imprisonment. King Thomas felt guilty, as, at heart, he was a kind and thoughtful man, who loved animals. As the years passed, he became more withdrawn and conflicted.

The once kind, humble princess was still angry with her father and her thoughts were dominated by trying to uncover the mystery of the dragon attack. Whenever Maranda could, and without her father realising, she spent time in the castle dungeons with the female dragon. She worked with her father's trusted knights and servants, who were all very fond

of her and so kept her secret. Together, they encouraged the dragon to keep moving and to flap her wings as much as possible in the cramped dungeon. Maranda also devoted any time she had to exercising her mind and body, by studying Tai Chi, sword play and survival strategies. While she trained herself harder and harder, her mother, Queen Jules, became increasingly worried about both her daughter and her husband.

"When are you two going to get along again, Thomas?" she asked.

"As soon as she puts that love for dragons behind her and focuses on her responsibilities to the kingdom!" King Thomas snapped back.

"She's loved dragons since she was five and has always worked with such passion and focus to develop her incredible knowledge of them," retorted his wife. "Do you really want to take that away from her? She is already anxious enough about becoming a queen and taking on the social responsibilities and weight of ruling the kingdom."

The king took a deep breath and said, "No, I'm sorry, Jules, what kind of father or king am I?"

The queen sat beside her husband. "I knew a brave knight and a noble warrior once," she said. "He didn't only stand up for himself, he also stood up for others. I didn't just marry him for his armour and his looks, I married him for his pure heart. And I believed in that warrior, I still do, and I know you'll find a way." King Thomas smiled, then hugged and kissed his queen.

While all that was going on, Princess Maranda was in the courtyard training herself for the challenges that awaited her beyond the castle walls. She exercised her muscles and developed her cunning with sword play, archery, agility and spear work. She also took the time to read in her room, to try to discover why the dragon might have attacked the fishing fleet. But eventually, she realised she wasn't going to find the answers she was seeking in books.

This is hopeless, she said to herself. *I'll never find any answers around here. If only there was a way*. She angrily tossed books and papers around the room and didn't bother to clean up. Great tears of sorrow began running down her cheeks.

Suddenly, a soft voice whispered from the shadows. "You are right not to judge the dragon for the fishing fleet attack."

Maranda, startled by the unexpected voice, looked

around her room. "Whoever's there, I'm in no mood for a lecture," she sobbed.

Out of the shadows appeared a glowing figure. "Don't despair, my child, for there is a larger game afoot," it said.

"Why can't everyone just leave me ALONE?" the princess cried in fury. Suddenly, as she threw a punch, the figure stopped her fist in midair.

"My name is Synder, a spirit of the forest." Synder put her hand on Maranda's forehead and showed her a vision. Maranda found herself in a different part of Muddle Worth, the place where the whistle-breath dragons had congregated after they were driven from the lake, to feed safely, away from human interference. The figure continued, "This is a place where the land's balance is shattering. Once there was a wetland as large as the eye could see. Now, since the volcano erupted, there is a land full of dried earth, dust and dead fish. The creatures that live here are suffering. The wrong of the dragon's capture has to be righted, a war has to be prevented from happening. If a war between kingdoms escalates, all life could be wiped out."

Maranda was curious and very worried about what Synder had said. "How can this damage be undone?" she asked.

Synder stared straight into her eyes and said, "Simple. You have to put your faith and trust in others; people will change if you give them a chance."

"But how can I trust other people if I can't even trust my father?" Maranda asked, feeling stressed all over.

Suddenly, Synder and Maranda sensed the queen coming. "Listen, Your Highness, you have a heart unlike any other; to save the wetlands and Muddle Worth, you must free the dragon." Before Maranda could open her mouth, Synder had disappeared.

"Maranda, sweetie," said the queen, "please may I come in?"

"Er, yeah, sure, Mum, come in," the princess said, pulling

herself together. As Queen Jules entered, Princess Maranda showed a cheesy smile (her way of keeping things together).

"Are you okay?" Queen Jules asked.

"Why yes, sure, Mum, how else would I feel?"

The queen wanted to talk to her daughter but was unsure how her girl would take the news she had to tell. "Listen, sweetheart, we need to talk," she said. They both sat on the princess' bed. "Honey, your father and I were talking. We both know that, if we don't do something about the dragon and the King of Dragon finds out that we have her captive, our kingdom could soon be at war with his." The princess agreed with her mother, but then her mother told her their solution…

"What, you expect me to become engaged to some snobbish prince who I don't even know?" Maranda exclaimed in surprise.

The queen tried to comfort her daughter, but, despite all her efforts, Maranda refused to agree to the engagement. The queen became very authoritative with the princess. "Now, listen here, young lady," she began. "If you don't marry Prince Delun, war with the Dragon Kingdom is a real threat, so swallow your pride. This is your duty, as a royal princess."

But the firm tone only made things worse, increasing Maranda's anxiety and making her angry. "Why can't you see that keeping the dragon captive is wrong? You have to let her go!" The princess yelled at her mother, tears streaming down her face. The queen didn't know how to answer and felt guilty about mishandling the situation and causing her daughter pain. She left the room, close to tears herself.

With that, Maranda couldn't take it any more. As soon as the castle was preparing for bed, she gathered her things into a travel bag and put on a warm cloak with a large hood. Using every bit of ingenuity she could muster, Maranda sneaked her way out of the window of her room and across the rooftops. But before she could flee over the castle walls, she had to find her way into the dungeon. She silently took out each of the guards along the way, rendering them unconscious using her training, and found her way to the large cell containing the female whistle-breath. Maranda took her hood down and looked at the dragon. She felt mournful to see the creature feeling so down and miserable. She could see that the dragon was covered in scars and lash marks from being confined. The few trusted knights who attended the dragon, with Maranda's help, had kept her well fed, but it was distressing to see the whistle-breath imprisoned. It appeared to Maranda that the magnificent creature she had admired from childhood had lost all hope.

She decided that enough was enough. She quietly took the cell keys from the hook next to the door and unlocked the dragon's cell. The dragon looked up from her sorrow. She perked up a little when she saw the princess walking up to her. Over the years, she had come to rely on the princess' kindness and gentle words, but even that didn't cure her bruises and stop the pain from the chains that bound her. Maranda was used to visiting the dragon with knight guards present, but she had never before been inside the cell, nor considered what she was planning on this visit. She stopped and breathed deeply to calm herself. The dragon, sensing a change in Maranda's mood, stared down and waited…

"Shh, it's all right, girl," Maranda whispered. "I won't harm you. In fact, I'm getting you out. I'm getting us both out." She tried to touch the dragon's nose, but the female growled distrustfully. "I know, I don't blame you, it's time the people responsible for treating you like this get what they deserve."

The princess gave the whistle-breath some space, understanding that she needed to earn the creature's trust even more to succeed in her plan. But she also knew she had no time to waste. So, after finding the right key on the chain, Maranda slowly reached up to unlock the dragon from her muzzle and chains. Instead of fighting back, the female whistle-breath started to calm down and, when they both looked into each other's eyes, they started to sense one another's souls.

The princess held up her hand. She didn't force the dragon to trust her, she just let it come to her willingly. Before Maranda knew it, the female dragon put her nose into the princess' hand. The whistle-breath gently sniffed Maranda's hand; from the scent, she could tell that Maranda meant no harm. Suddenly, both Maranda and the dragon heard the guards coming.

"Listen," whispered the princess, "we don't have much time. You may not know me well, but, if we're getting out of here, we have to work together. Do you understand?"

The captain of the knight guards and six of his men ran over to the cell. Maranda quickly pulled the hood over her head, so they couldn't recognise her.

"Hey, you, get away from the beast!" bellowed the captain. But, just before the knights could contain her, Maranda climbed onto the dragon's back. The dragon growled and let out shards of ice.

"INCOMING!" cried the captain. But it was too late, a carpet of ice shards froze the guards in place. The blast from her breath shattered the bars of the dragon's cell and the pair burst out and began charging through the dungeon corridors.

"Do you trust me?" Maranda said into the dragon's ear. The dragon nodded. "Then follow my voice!" the princess urged. With her help, the princess and the dragon navigated through the catacombs, slamming into every guard that got in their way. The captain pursued them until they reached an exit. "Can you still fly?" Maranda asked. As they reached the exit, the dragon burst through, spread her wings and took off into the night sky, with the princess hanging on, answering

Maranda's question and leaving the guards baffled and bruised.

As the castle faded from sight, Maranda knew there was no turning back; they had a job to do.

CHAPTER 8

Found out the Truth

Richard was by now also sixteen. He was becoming a fine young man and Chester had grown into a strong, capable, playful, four-year-old colt. The two of them remained firm friends.

Richard continued doing his chores with his mum and dad and, in his spare time, regularly went to the field to check up on Chester. "Hey, buddy," he would say, "would you like an apple?" Chester had learned that apples strengthen the

bond between a horse and his master.

One day, after Chester had munched through his apple, Richard asked, "So, what shall we do today?"

Chester thought and then started to bend down. Richard couldn't tell what he was doing at first, then realised that his friend wanted him to climb on his back to ride. Richard knew his dad planned to start training Chester for riding soon, so would not want Richard to go bareback riding before then. He said nervously to Chester, "Um, I don't know, pal, what if I fall off, what will Dad say?" But Chester wouldn't take no for an answer. "All right, if you insist," Richard said, and climbed onto Chester's back.

When Richard got on, he was about to tell Chester to start slow, but the colt was so full of energy, he took off like the wind.

"Woooooah," cried Richard. The two of them ran over the fields and across the river. "Not too far from home, boy, I have to be back for lunch and more chores," said Richard. Chester's mother watched and smiled, seeing her son playing with the boy. Fortunately, Richard and Chester were safely back in the field and Richard had climbed down off Chester's back when Farmer Rosemary appeared in the farmyard.

"Richard, come on, we have to take the milk, eggs and vegetables to market," he called.

"I've got to go, buddy; have fun and enjoy yourself," Richard said to Chester. Chester was put back into his stall, while Sophie was attached to a waggon to take Farmer Rosemary and Richard to market with the produce, milk and eggs. Chester waited, waited and waited, but he couldn't help pawing the ground with his hooves in excitement. It was a bit difficult because the colt had lots of energy in his system and not enough patience.

At the chicken coop, Wisdom had also grown into a young, strong adolescent dragon, alongside his brother Tonto, now an impressive young cockerel. One day, they were hanging around the yard, feeling a bit bored and trying to decide what to do next. Wisdom started practising his concealment skills, annoying Tonto by sneaking up behind him.

Suddenly, a pack of three wolves sprang from the bushes. The lead wolf, Snare, caught the young cockerel by the throat and started dragging him away. "Wisdom, help," he croaked.

"Shut your beak, lunch, or we'll shut it for you," snarled Snare. The second wolf licked his chops.

"Oh boy, I can't wait to get my jaws into some chicken flesh," he said excitedly.

Before they could proceed with lunch, Wisdom, who was still concealed, swished his tail and tripped up both wolves, making Snare drop Tonto. Wisdom revealed himself and cried, "Hey, leave my brother alone and pick on someone your own size." Snare just laughed, while the rest of the pack cowered behind him, as they had never seen a dragon before and were frightened.

Snare turned to his pack members and snarled, "What's the matter? Haven't you bozos ever seen a dragon before? Boy, does this dragon nobody want to play hero or what?" Turning to Wisdom, he continued, "We don't have time for your games, kid, we've got lunch to stuff, so get out of the way."

But Wisdom wouldn't move from his spot. The wolves were starting to get annoyed.

"Hey, are you asking for trouble? We said, 'get out of the way'!"

Still, Wisdom would not move from where he was standing. "No," he said, full of determination.

"No?" growled Snare.

The other chickens heard the commotion and so did Chester. The chickens looked through the fence to see Wisdom having a standoff with the wolf pack.

"The only way I'll ever move from this spot and stop protecting my friend is if you make me," Wisdom snorted.

Snare stepped forward and stared the young dragon straight in the eyes. "Out of my way, boy, or there'll be trouble."

Wisdom grabbed hold of Snare's head and tossed him around like a rag doll, surprising the chickens and himself with his strength.

"You just bit me?" snarled Snare. "Boys, let's show this nobody the consequences of his actions."

Willow was getting worried. "Run, Wisdom, run!" she cried. But Wisdom would not give up on Tonto. Two of the wolves charged, while the third watched Tonto. They attacked him from every angle. The young dragon used his tail like a mace and barrel-rolled them off his back. But no matter how hard he tried, the wolves were starting to overpower Wisdom.

"Go, Tonto, get back to Mum!" Wisdom cried. But Tonto would not leave his brother.

Snare grinned at Tonto and said to the other wolves, "Finish this kid off, the young rooster is mine to eat." The other chickens waited for the worst to happen. Suddenly, out of nowhere, ice came blasting out of Wisdom's mouth, freezing the second and third wolves in their path. Wisdom followed up with a tail swish and a head butt, knocking them unconscious.

With three kicks to the stall door, Chester, who had seen the whole thing, escaped and hurried towards the commotion.

"Enough!" yelled Snare. "I'm gonna have chicken for lunch, no matter how much it hurts m…" But before he could finish his sentence, ice breath froze him in place too and then a tail swipe sent Snare flying into the barn wall.

When Chester arrived, all he could see were the three wolves slowly staggering to their feet and limping away towards the woods, ice everywhere and Wisdom gazing after them looking victorious.

"Beat it and never return!" Wisdom yelled after them and let out a long, shrill cry. It echoed throughout the farm and the valley. Even Mrs Rosemary heard it inside the farmhouse.

"What the heck was that?" she said in surprise.

Tonto ran to his brother's side. "Was that ice coming out of your mouth?" he asked.

"Wis, that was awesome, pal," said Chester excitedly. "How did you do that?"

"I don't know," answered Wisdom, as questions about his life, his powers and his true identity flooded his brain.

Later, Willow saw Wisdom sitting in the corner of the farmyard. He was contemplating his true identity. "Son, what's wrong?" she asked gently.

"I'm starting to think that I'm not really a chicken. So, what am I?" asked the young dragon.

Willow gulped because she knew that Wisdom was entitled to ask where he came from and what species he really was. She took a deep breath and said, "Wisdom, walk with me please, there's something I should've told you long ago."

With that, she took Wisdom around the farm, told him that he was a dragon and that he was found as an egg in the river and rescued by Chester. Wisdom was surprised by the fact that he wasn't a part of the farm.

"So, I'm not your real son?" he asked.

"You'll always be my son, Wisdom, and I love you no matter what."

But Wisdom had more questions about his past. "May I talk to Chester please?" Willow nodded and Wisdom climbed over the fence and into the field.

When he came across Chester, the two of them started talking at once.

"Hi Wis, have you come to have fun?" Chester asked.

"No, I've come to find out about my past," said Wisdom. Chester didn't know what his friend was getting at, but he went along with it anyway.

"Why did you save me?" Wisdom asked him.

Suddenly, Chester realised what Wisdom was asking, so he told him. "I don't know, maybe something inside me just couldn't let you perish when you were an egg."

Wisdom felt huge gratitude to Chester for saving his life. "Thank you, pal, I owe you my life. But I have so many questions. Like how did I get into the river? Why don't I like chicken feed? Where did I come from and who am I?" Chester was the closest friend Wisdom had, but not even he had the answers to Wisdom's questions.

Wisdom climbed onto the barn roof and looked out at the valley, still pondering questions about his past.

Tonto flew up to the roof and sat beside his brother. "Hey, bro, are you okay?"

Wisdom shook his head. "I always wanted to know about my past and who I really am, but I'm also not so sure about where it might lead." Tonto recognised that Wisdom had some thinking to do and knew this was not the time for jokes, so he decided to give his brother some space.

Chester and Willow were very concerned about Wisdom and what he was going through. "Do you think Wisdom's going to be all right?" Chester asked. Willow could only give Chester the look of 'I hope so'.

Sooner or later, Wisdom will figure out what he is, where he came from, what he is capable of and what part he will play in the future of Muddle Worth.

CHAPTER 9

How to Train Your Horse

Soon the day came for Richard to leave school and to start work as a full-time farm assistant for his dad, so he could learn the ropes of farming. The day after school ended, the farmer asked his son to join him in the stable yard. "Richard, I've got a surprise for you, my boy. Today is the day that I'm starting to train a few young horses for riding and working and I would like you to help."

Richard was often anxious about surprises, but, as he had been thinking about training Chester for months, this time he felt very excited.

"Steady on, son, it'll take some time," his father said. "First, I need you to fetch Chester from the field and bring him into the yard."

"Don't worry, Dad, I'll have my friend in the yard before you can say sunshine."

"Sunshine!" chuckled the farmer and he and his son started laughing.

Richard, still chuckling to himself, set off to fetch Chester, calling as he walked. In the far field, Chester was trying out his running speed and endurance. His long, golden mane flew in the wind as he ran. When he reached a rocky platform, he reared up and whinnied with joy. His mum smiled and shook her head. She was proud and delighted that her son had grown up to be strong, handsome and free as the wind. Chester was proving himself to be faster than all the other horses on the farm.

The sound of Richard calling his friend's name was usually enough to bring the stallion back, but Chester was too far away to hear him. When Chester didn't appear, Sophie whinnied loudly, quickly bringing Chester galloping back.

When Chester saw Richard with a halter in his hand, something inside told him that it was time for training. He ran back to the fence as fast as his muscular legs could carry him.

"Hey, buddy," said Richard. "It's time to train you to be a work horse." Chester couldn't wait to start his training. Richard put the halter over the stallion's head and started leading him towards the yard. Then Farmer Rosemary showed Chester the bridle. Chester thought it looked a little like a halter, but noticed one big difference, a piece of metal holding the bridle together: THE BIT!

"Son," said Farmer Rosemary. "I need you to step back, watch and learn. I don't want you to get bitten or kicked; horses can be very unpredictable."

"I can calm him down for you, Father," Richard insisted. But the farmer gave him a stern look, so Richard obeyed.

When Farmer Rosemary tried slowly putting the bridle over Chester's head, the stallion backed away. "I'm sorry, boy," said the farmer gently to Chester. "I understand you're scared, but that's why we are going to practise this slowly. It's all going to be okay." Reassuring with his kind, soft voice, the farmer slowly and gently began to put the bridle onto Chester's head. But Chester was surprised when his master put the bit into his mouth. The taste was so bad and the metal so hard that Chester snorted and tried to spit it out. Richard quickly held out an apple to his friend to persuade him that a bit could be okay and not to spit it out.

The next part was the saddle. The farmer told Richard to rush to the tack room and fetch one. He came back with a large saddle. They tried it on, but it felt uncomfortable on Chester's shoulders and back. Father and son both realised that it didn't fit properly. So, they put Chester's halter over his bridle, tied him to a strong fence post and set off towards the stables. The farmer turned to his son and said, "Remember, the right sized saddle is one that is not too long or too short, gives space for the horse to move freely and makes good contact along the horse's back."

After checking through every saddle they could find, Farmer Rosemary found the one he was looking for, right at the back of the storeroom. "This saddle belonged to Chester's father, Flame," he told his son. "I haven't seen it in years." The farmer blew and rubbed the dust off the saddle and began to tell Richard some more. "This saddle has history written all over it, son. You see, a long time ago, way before I became a farmer in Bear Kingdom, I was a knight of the Wolf Kingdom. Flame was more than just a noble steed, he was my very best friend. We worked together, trained together and fought together." While walking back to Chester, Farmer Rosemary kept telling his son about the glory days he and Flame had together. Chester was listening intently to every word, and he was excited to hear that he was wearing his old man's saddle.

Farmer Rosemary showed Richard how to lunge and lead a horse. "Let me tell you something that my father taught me. A man is only as good as the horse he rides. Take care of the horse, the horse will take care of you."

Richard never forgot that advice from his father. Neither did Chester. Chester also had to learn how to pick up his feet for filing, how to stand still to be tacked up and how to work with a rider. Both boy and horse found out that there was much to learn.

"What's next, Dad?" asked Richard.

"Before we ride Chester out of the field, we have to take him to see a blacksmith; he needs some horseshoes. Now, tack up Sophie, my boy, and we'll hitch her to the waggon; we're off to town to see the blacksmith." Chester still had his father's saddle and bridle on. His two masters got the waggon and Sophie ready for the road. Sophie had years of experience of blacksmith visits, so she gently reassured Chester that everything would be fine.

After kissing Mrs Rosemary goodbye, father and son hitched both horses to the waggon. Chester had no idea how to pull a waggon, but his mother was right next to him to help guide him. She was a good, calm and hard-working horse and she showed him how to be one with the waggon. "You're doing well, my son; they say the more you work hard and well, the better humans will treat you."

Chester was confused. "But I thought our farmer treats all us animals well," he said.

Sophie nodded her head and then shrugged her shoulders. "Yes, but I must warn you, not all humans are as kind as our master and his son," she said.

On the waggon, Richard had a lot of questions for his father. "I don't get it, Dad, how come you didn't tell me you used to be a knight?" he asked. Farmer Rosemary was starting to worry that he had told Richard too much and that his son might develop ideas of becoming a knight himself and wouldn't come home safely from battle.

"Son, we have a job to do, let's not discuss the past today, okay?" said Samuel kindly, but making it clear that the subject was closed.

At Roland Town, the farmer asked the blacksmith for his finest horseshoes. The blacksmith agreed. Chester looked anxiously back at his mother, and she gave him a nod of encouragement. With that, Chester took a deep breath and allowed Richard and the farmer to take him into the blacksmith's shack. The blacksmith started to pick up each hoof, front and back. First, he picked the dirt from out of the underparts of the hooves and then filed the edges and measured the hooves. To Chester it all tickled him and felt strange, but he kept it together. Then the blacksmith heated and shaped each iron shoe in turn with a hammer, while Richard stayed by Chester's side to calm him down. "Well done, boy," he said, comfortingly.

"You're doing great," the blacksmith said, pressing the hot shoes one by one against Chester's hooves to check the fit. After cooling the shoes in cold water, the blacksmith nailed them to Chester's hooves. He explained to Richard that the heat and nails didn't hurt Chester, as horses' hooves don't have nerve endings.

Farmer Rosemary stayed to pay the blacksmith. Richard took Chester outside and was just about to hitch the horses to the waggon, when he heard a loud cry. Richard turned and, across the square, saw a frightened man being bullied by a giant, angry man. Richard knew in his heart that he couldn't stand by and watch others being hurt.

"Can you keep Dad busy, while I take care of business?" he asked Chester. Chester looked and guessed what his boy was going to do. He supported his friend, but he was also concerned.

By the time Farmer Rosemary came back to the waggon, all he saw were the horses, but no Richard in sight. The farmer sighed.

"Richard, where are you now?" he called, followed by a muttered, "Where could that boy have gone off to?"

The horses looked at each other and shook their heads. "Myrrh!" they snorted in return.

On the other side of the square, the giant barked aggressively.

"Give me your bread right now or I'm going to kick your pathetic heads into the ground."

The man replied defiantly, "Why don't you leave us alone?"

The giant had grabbed him by the neck and was about to squeeze when Richard stepped in. "Hey, put him down," he yelled.

But the giant just chuckled and ignored him. "Go tend to chores, munchkin, or I'll break you."

But Richard wouldn't back down. He was holding a pitchfork in one hand and started to walk towards the giant. "Maybe you didn't hear me, I said put him down." Then, with the words out of his mouth, he stabbed the fork into the giant's left leg.

The big man gave a roar of pain, then turned to face Richard. "You should've stayed out of my way, toadstool," he snarled.

Richard was beginning to wish he had minded his own business. But every time the giant laid blows on him, Richard kept getting back up. The giant couldn't believe his eyes, nor could the gathering crowd.

"You just don't know when to quit, do you?" yelled the giant.

Richard looked the giant bully straight in the eyes and said, "Do your worst."

The giant was about to deliver another blow when a metal pole struck his fist. It was Farmer Rosemary. "Enough," he snorted loudly. "Step away from my son and walk away!"

"Out of my way, old man," the giant snarled. He tried to push the farmer away, but Farmer Rosemary wasn't going to make it easy. As the giant charged, the farmer thrust out his pole and tripped him up. He landed heavily, letting out an agonised yell. Farmer Rosemary turned, offered the giant his hand to help him up and then firmly told the giant to go and never return.

Back at the waggon, Chester saw what was happening.

"Hey, Mother, when you said that other humans are not always as kind as our masters, you weren't kidding."

"What were you thinking, son, that man could've beaten you to your last breath!" Farmer Rosemary cried, looking really worried.

Richard was leaning on his father's shoulder, feeling battered and bruised. "I couldn't just stand by and watch those good people suffer at the hands of a bully." He groaned.

"Son, there are people who handle this sort of thing," said his father.

"Yeah, but where were they when it happened?" Richard asked anxiously, trembling from the shock of the experience.

Farmer Rosemary (who was also frightened but trying not to show it) just said, "Enough, we can't discuss this now, let's get you back home and make sure you're okay."

On the way home, Chester was worried about Richard's condition. Not only that, the iron shoes made his feet feel stiff and heavy. Sophie tried to comfort him the best she could. "Don't worry, Chester, it took me days until I grew used to horseshoes."

"It's not just that," Chester said. "I'm also concerned about Richard; do you think he did the right thing defending those people?"

His mother looked concerned and started to explain. "Standing up for others, yes, but he has to understand that violence will never solve anything," she said. "I need you to promise me that you will watch over Richard and remind him that violence isn't the answer; promise me, my son."

Promises are often hard to keep, but Chester knew that what his mother was asking was very important. He was unsure and scared that he would mess up the promise, but the worried and concerned look in his mother's eyes persuaded him. He took a deep breath, looked her in the eyes and said, "I promise, I will watch over Richard with my life." Then the two horses lovingly rubbed each other's heads.

The next morning, Richard was told to muck out the cows and clear up around the barn. His parents had grounded him because of his reckless actions the previous day. He wasn't allowed to visit the horses, run around the field nor have fun until he'd totally finished his chores. While he worked, his mind wandered and he began dreaming of becoming a knight like his father.

On the other side of the farm, it was time for Chester to learn how to carry a person on his back. So, Farmer Rosemary saddled and bridled Chester and reassured him that everything was going to be okay. His hands were as soft as hay in a stall.

"It's going to be okay, my boy," said the farmer softly. "Do you trust me?" Chester wasn't sure what to expect, but he pointed his ears forward, showing the farmer that he trusted him. Samuel put his left foot into the stirrup and climbed carefully onto Chester's back. He was a bit heavy, but Chester soon adjusted to having a human on his back. They took a gentle walk around the farm. Farmer Rosemary was so kind and content just to let the chestnut horse walk at his own pace.

"Isn't this a good place, boy? I wish my son could see this for himself, wouldn't you agree?" Chester whinnied in agreement. Things were going smoothly, so the farmer decided to have some fun. "Okay, boy, are you ready to fly?" he asked. Chester was so excited he whinnied loudly. The farmer called out, "LET EM FLY, YA!" prompting Chester to take off and run like the wind. The young horse felt freer than he had ever done in his life. It was fun, until Farmer Rosemary pulled up gradually on the reins, signalling Chester to slow down.

Finally, the farmer got off Chester's back and led him back to the farmyard. "Did you have fun today, fella?" he asked playfully. On the way back to the farm's main gate, they found Bonnie and Richard waiting.

"How was he, love?" Mrs Rosemary asked keenly.

"Well, my love," said the farmer, "he runs faster and for longer than any I've ever seen. His coat shines like the sun, he's as free as the wind and he has a lot of spirit."

"May I cuddle him, Father?" asked Richard.

The farmer wasn't going to let cross feelings from the previous day get in the way, so he kindly offered Chester to Richard. "He deserves it, hon," he said to his wife. "Richard has worked hard with Chester, so he should be rewarded."

"You're right, sweetie," Mrs Rosemary whispered to her husband. "Those two are adorable together, but, who knows, we may have to sell Chester if the farm's finances don't improve."

CHAPTER 10

Spread Your Wings

While Chester was training to become a work horse, Wisdom still had many questions about his identity and his past.

"Now I know I'm not a chicken, I'm thinking that clearly I don't even belong here," he said. "What should I do about it?" he asked Devon, the wise old farm donkey. Now, nobody has answers for everything, but Devon gave Wisdom his thoughts.

"The way I see it, sonny, when I have questions, I take a deep breath, start at the beginning, replay my steps and, before you know it, the answer shortly finds itself. Try it if you can."

Wisdom didn't know what to expect, but he tried it out anyway. Tonto was standing with him. Wisdom closed his eyes, took a breath and replayed his steps through his childhood. As he kept replaying in his mind, something incredible began to happen. His wings started to move, then flap and, the more Wisdom replayed his steps, the more his wings flapped. When he opened his eyes, to his surprise, he saw his feet weren't touching the ground. The other animals couldn't believe their eyes either.

"What happened?" Wisdom asked in surprise.

"You're flying, bro!" Tonto cried.

"How do you feel, honey?" asked Willow.

"Startled, but awesome," whooped Wisdom.

"Why don't you take yourself for a test flight?" asked Bessie, one of the cows.

"But be careful, son!" called Willow.

Wisdom was so excited to try out his wings, he shot up high into the sky. He climbed higher and higher until he was soaring above the clouds. He was amazed and nervous because he had never before been up so high. He started exploring the cloud realm, passing and startling some wild geese on their way south. Suddenly, he realised that he needed to get home.

"How do I get back down?" he cried aloud, feeling rather scared.

A voice spoke softly from all around the sky. "Dragon, I need you to remain calm and listen to what I'm about to tell you," it said.

Wisdom was terrified. "Who said that and what did you call me?" he asked in fright.

"Do not be frightened," the voice continued, "I am Synder, and I am here to tell you that you are not just any dragon, you're one of a unique kind called whistle-breaths."

"I don't know what you're talking about, and I don't have time for this." But before Wisdom could fly off, Synder appeared in front of his nose.

"You will listen," she said firmly, but gently. Wisdom was both startled and amazed at what he saw. It was a being unlike any he had ever seen. Even though it was blocking his way, Wisdom took a deep breath and composed himself, his mind filled with one simple question.

"What are you?" stuttered Wisdom.

"What I am does not matter, just know that you will shortly be caught up in a battle you've yet to understand. A war that could consume and destroy the balance of Muddle Worth, unless someone has the courage to stop it."

"And why should I believe anything you say?" Wisdom asked, looking very concerned. Synder continued to tell Wisdom that, four years earlier, the Bear Kingdom had captured a dragon, after she froze their fishing fleet and stole their fish. The previous week, news of the capture had finally reached the King of Dragon. He was now furious and threatening war against the Bear Kingdom, if the dragon was not returned to him safe and sound.

"You mean, there are other creatures like me out there?" Wisdom asked.

Synder nodded. "To find the answers to the questions you've been asking yourself, you must first fight for your land. I will soon send you a message to go to Havoc Creek, where you will learn more about your past and prepare yourself for the challenges ahead. You won't be fighting alone. An alliance will be formed, answers will be found and wrongs will have to be righted."

Then, just like that, Synder disappeared. Wisdom wasn't sure what Synder meant, but as they say, the sooner you start your journey, the sooner the answers will find you. He took a long flight to ponder what Synder had said. Suddenly, visions filled his mind: he saw knights in battle crying out and yelling and heard the sound of another dragon in pain. When he finally returned home, the animals were gathered around to hear how his flight went. Even Chester had taken time off from his training to see his friend fly.

"Hey, how did your flight go, bro?" asked Tonto.

"Did you find another world above the clouds, pal?" asked Chester. But Wisdom's head was so full of visions and unexpected information, he barely even looked at his friends.

The animals' faces changed from excited to concerned, because, to them, Wisdom was still a part of the farm family, no matter how different he was.

Chester said to Tonto, "You and I have to talk to him."

When Willow overheard what Chester said, she advised, "Take it easy on him."

They found Wisdom in the barn, still in thinking mode.

"What's up, bro?" asked Tonto.

"Don't know, the clouds maybe," Wisdom retorted.

"If you want to tell us what's going on, we're right here and listening," said Chester comfortingly. Wisdom was unsure; if he did tell his friends, there was no telling how they would react. But he took a deep breath and started to speak.

After he told them that Synder had warned him about the upcoming war, he waited nervously for the reply.

"So, a glowing figure came out of nowhere and told you that there's going to be a war between kingdoms?" Tonto asked, trying to put the pieces together.

"Yeah!" said Wisdom. Tonto laughed, but Chester didn't think it was funny, so he stepped in.

"What Tonto is trying to say is, 'we believe you'," he said.

"Synder also said that I can't take on this journey alone. I need followers and allies," Wisdom said. Then he had an idea.

"Hey what do you guys say, will you support me to follow my destiny out into the big wide world? Tonto, will you please stay here and look after Mum?"

Chester and Tonto looked at each other, then made a decision. "We may not be related," said Tonto, "but, as your brother, Wis, it is my job to support you. I will stay here, look after Mum and wait for your return."

"We should all watch each other's backs," said Chester. "Wis, you and I may need Richard on this adventure in the future. So, are we ready for whatever lies ahead?" The others nodded. Wisdom put his paw in the middle, Chester put his hoof on Wisdom's hand and Tonto put his right claw in too. And on that day, they made promises to have each other's backs, by supporting each other and working together throughout the challenges ahead.

CHAPTER 11

The Workout

Richard continued dreaming of becoming a knight and of making the world a better place. He worked hard, using his autistic focusing powers to help him learn how to manage the farm, build his strength and train in knightly combat skills. He designed training equipment and basic weapons from anything he could lay his hands on. He lifted hay bales and did pull-ups and press-ups in the barn, dragged really heavy loads, practised his sword play, chopped wood with an axe and rode Chester every chance he had, to develop his riding skills.

The more the young man trained and pushed himself, the more concerned his parents became about his obsession and increasing isolation. As the weeks passed, the farmer and his wife knew there was a question they had to face. Normally, any parent would be proud to see their child grow up, but it's also scary to let them go. Samuel and Bonnie debated and argued for many days. After a particularly lengthy discussion one day, Samuel and Bonnie came to a decision, which they agreed to tell Richard the following day.

The next morning, the family gathered for a bacon and egg breakfast. There was tension in the air and silence fell, before Farmer Rosemary looked at his son and said, "Richard, we have to talk."

Normally, Richard would be concerned at that remark, as

he always feared unexpected news, but he took a deep breath and said, "I'm listening, Dad." His father told him that he and his mum, like all parents, wanted to protect Richard, but they also wanted him to be happy. They realised that he was sad and frustrated, which was distressing for them too. So, Samuel told Richard, if becoming a knight was what he really wanted, then he and Richard's mum would support him and he would consider personally training him. Richard leaped up, smiled and hugged his dad and then his mum. He could hardly believe his ears; he was over the moon.

"First of all, doing your chores is considered part of your training," said the farmer. "Chores are what keep a man and woman honest and give you discipline; your mother taught me that when we met. Remember with age comes experience and more freedom to make your own choices, but also with age comes great responsibility."

Richard never forgot his father's advice, because you never knew when it might come in handy during dark times. His training began. His father helped him combine training with his chores around the farm. They ploughed fields, lifted hay bales, practised press-ups, pull-ups and riding skills and learned how to carve better practice weapons. Then Farmer Rosemary taught his son the basics of combat and defence, using the wooden practice swords, shields and lances they had carved.

Chester trained hard with his friend and he and Richard became a very skilled mounted team. Chester also watched his friend train and work throughout the days and weeks, often late into the night, on his unmounted combat skills and his strength. Chester felt proud of his young master's progress. The farmer and his wife were also proud of the way their son was working hard and moving forward.

One day, during training, Farmer Rosemary said to his son, "The keys to being a knight are patience, nobility, discipline and learning defence strategies to give you the ability to survive. To be a knight, you must first control yourself from the inside and out. Now, attack me if you can."

Richard tried attacking, but Samuel kept on dodging and deflecting, time after time.

Richard grew increasingly frustrated.

"Easy, easy," said Samuel. "You can't let your anger get you down. If it takes over your system, you could lose control and be injured, or even end up dead. The question is, no matter how many times you get hit, can you get back up?"

Richard carried on training; sure, he failed a few times, sure he was frustrated, but his dad reminded him about control and the importance of moving forward.

While Samuel was talking with Richard, on the other side of the farm, Wisdom was looking out at the view. Willow approached him and sat beside her son.

"I don't know about you, Mum," said Wisdom, "but, somewhere out there, are a lot of adventures to be had."

Willow sighed and said, "Son, a little advice from a mother hen: what you're searching for is not out there, but inside. I want you to know that, whoever this dragon will become, he will change the world. So, I want you to promise me that you will be careful and true to yourself." Wisdom smiled and put his head close to Willow's.

That very night, it was time for this young dragon to go out into the big world, discover the secret of his past and to experience new things along the way. While the humans were sleeping, the animals gathered in the barn to see Wisdom off.

Jackson stood on a pile of hay bales to make an announcement. "My friends, neighbours and family, we are gathered today to say goodbye to an honorary member of our farmyard family. When Wisdom came into our lives, I wanted nothing to do with him because he was different. But if Wisdom hadn't been there for his brother, Tonto would have been wolf food. It's time that we let him spread his wings and see the world. Wisdom, no matter what happens, I want you to know that you will always be a part of our family."

Jackson insisted that Wisdom came up to say a few words to the barnyard. "I'm not one for making long speeches," Wisdom said, "but I will say this: while some of you see me as an outsider, others see me as a special part of the family. I wish I could stay, but I have to find out where I came from and who I really am. Before I leave, I just want to say that, whether the farmer and his family are around or not, I'll come back and visit."

Wisdom embraced each animal around the farmyard to thank them for taking care of and looking out for him. He turned to Willow. "Thank you for loving me as your son. No matter who I am or where I go, you will always be my mother," he said.

Willow cried and hugged him. "And you will always be in my heart. Don't forget to be true to yourself."

Wisdom turned to Tonto and Chester and said, "I guess this is it."

"Hey, this isn't goodbye," said Chester. "After all, we promised we'd look out for each other."

"Yeah, we're a team, even when we're apart," said Tonto. "You know I wish I could go with you."

"Don't worry, I know you support me and I agree someone's got to look after our mother while I'm gone," Wisdom reassured his brother.

The friends high-fived each other and, just like that, Wisdom took one last look at his adopted family and friends, then he spread his wings, made a running start and took off into the night. The animals were very sad to see him go, but they understood his desire to find his own way in the big world.

CHAPTER 12

Princess in Hiding

While Richard was working hard at his training and Wisdom was discovering more about his powers and his destiny, at the Bear Kingdom, the king and queen were increasingly worried about their daughter.

"She should've known better than to run away," King Thomas said. "I mean, she could've told me if she was unhappy..."

"She tried, but you weren't listening to her," Queen Jules interrupted. "And now our baby girl is out there by herself. We have to find her."

A messenger came into the throne room with an urgent message. "Your majesties, I bring news from the Dragon Kingdom, the king is furious that you have been keeping a whistle-breath captive all these years. He has declared that, if the creature they respect is harmed or killed, then we are at war."

The king and queen looked at each other and the king made a decision. "This is my fault, Jules," he said to his wife. "I realise now that if anyone should find our daughter and bring her home, it's me."

Queen Jules was unsure about her husband going out there alone, but the king put his arms around her, hugged her and told her everything would be fine. "Bring our baby girl home, I believe in you," she said.

King Thomas put on his armour, saddled and then mounted his horse.

"I'm going to find the princess and bring her home. In the meantime, I'm leaving my beloved queen in charge of the kingdom until I return," he told his castle guard patrols. "If I don't bring her back, we are going to have a major war on our hands. Carry on." With that, he rode out through the castle gate, along the peninsula away from the lake and out towards the forest.

Be safe, my love, the queen said to herself.

When Maranda had fled the castle, she and the female dragon had flown as far as the dragon's wings could take her. They had landed in a gorge surrounded by dense forest. "Thank you for that huge effort, girl," said Maranda. "Listen, we can't be seen together, okay? I need you to lay low until we can find a way to stop the war." The whistle-breath wasn't sure what war she meant, but the serious look in the princess' eyes was clear, so the dragon took off and flew away to her cave above Havoc Creek. From that moment, Maranda was no longer a princess of Bear, but a fugitive on the run. She disappeared aimlessly into the forest; she knew that she was going to have to tough it out, if she ever wanted to see her parents again.

Maranda ran as deep as she could into the forest, until finally she came to a cave suited to house a runaway young girl. But the cave was occupied by a brown bear with her cubs. At first, the mother bear was very aggressive to the stranger's presence. Maranda was scared and had no idea how to react. She kept her distance and chose a secluded part of the cave away from the bear family, where she lit a fire to warm herself up. The reality of running away from her family, her kingdom and her responsibilities began to sink in. She began to realise that, even though she had helped the dragon escape, there could still be a war. She felt anxious, afraid and alone.

By the time the king set out to search for his daughter, many weeks had passed and Maranda had settled down to a life on the land: running, climbing, carving and hunting to survive. She designed her own bow and arrows, started studying and learning how to defend herself and how to harness her skills through trial and error. She was even starting to make friends with the spirits of the forest besides Synder. But she wasn't just planning to use her skills to survive in the wild. When the time was right, she was determined to return and stop the war.

Her father, the king, searched and searched deep into the forest for several days, but to no avail. He knew that his kingdom needed him, so very reluctantly, he rode back in the direction of Bear Castle, unaware that he was being watched by his own daughter.

Back at Rosemary Farm, things were going from bad to worse; the farm was losing money, even though the farmer

was working as hard as he possibly could, often through the night. His wife was concerned about the farm, but, most importantly of all, she was very concerned about her husband's welfare. "I just can't bear to see you exhaust yourself, my love," she reassured him.

For Richard, this was his first real taste of hardship. He stood at the farm door with his mum, as Samuel headed out to start work. "How is he?" he asked his mum.

Bonnie tried to put on a brave face. "Your father's fine; exhausted, but fine."

But even Richard could see that his father was in a bad way, so he followed his dad into the yard, calling after him, "Look, Dad, wait, you really need to rest. If you don't, you won't have enough energy to work."

"I'll rest when the farm is saved," Samuel replied, stubborn as always.

"Now listen," Bonnie stepped in, "if there's one thing we as a family do, it's push through together, no matter the challenge."

From the stable, Chester was listening to the conversation the farmer and his family were having. He turned to his mother in the next stall and said, "Mum, do you think that we'll lose the farm, if the farmer can't earn enough to pay the bills?"

Sophie could see that her son was scared and unsure, so she comforted him. "Hey, chin up, my boy," she smiled, trying to keep a brave face. "If there's one thing my mother taught me, it is that home is more than just a roof over your head. Remember, no matter how far from home you go, the love we all share will stay forever."

Richard thought about the situation as he worked hard with his father during the day. He was concerned about his family's farm and his parents trying to pay the feed, vets' and other bills. Finally, he had an idea that would change the course of his life. In the evening, as they all sat down wearily to eat, he told his parents that he would leave the farm and go to Bear Castle to apply to become a knight to earn enough money to save the farm. His mother was unsure about her baby boy leaving the safety of home and ending up in a strange, unfamiliar place, but his father understood that the time had come to let his son go. So, they both agreed that Richard would go and earn money to try to save the farm.

The next day, Richard and his father got Chester out of the stable, groomed and fed him and then tacked him up.

"I'm proud of you, son, you're becoming a man," his father said. The farmer then turned to Chester. "I trust you to take care of our son and remind him who he really is and what we stand for," he said.

Chester snorted in agreement. Bonnie kissed Richard on the forehead and Chester on the snout to wish them luck. But she was scared of losing her little boy. "For years, I've been taking care of my little boy, making sure he's loved and that he feels like he belongs. Now that you're going out into the world, I'm afraid of what the big world will do to you," she said. "So, I need you to promise me that you will take care of that little boy for me, give him a reason to keep going, help him never to give up on what he is fighting for and make sure he stays true to himself. Promise me, Richard," she said, fighting back the tears.

Richard took a deep breath, looked his mother in the eye and said, "I promise."

His mother smiled and hugged him tight. Then Farmer Rosemary came over with a chain mail vest. "Bonnie, I'd like to have a moment with our son, please," he said kindly, and his wife stepped aside.

"Son, I want you to have this."

"What is this, Dad?" Richard asked.

"This vest has protected me throughout many dark times.

It was mine, now it's yours to wear. It will protect you in your darkest times. Don't forget what a knight stands for: honour. I love you, my boy." Richard gave his father a big hug to say that he loved him back.

After saying goodbye, Richard climbed onto Chester's saddle. "Come on, Chester, to Bear Castle," he said. He then gently kicked his friend to make him walk.

"I'll make you guys proud," he called back.

"I know you will," the farmer said softly. And just like that, the two friends went out onto the road.

CHAPTER 13
Answers Will Come

The same day that Richard left Rosemary Farm, Wisdom received a message from Synder telling him to go to the Havoc Creek canyon, just as she had warned. Wisdom was flying to Havoc Creek as quickly as his wings would carry him, when all of a sudden, the heavens opened. He pushed onwards, despite the lightning and thunder thrashing around him.

What am I doing? he asked himself. I'm far away from home, I have no idea what I'm looking for and I must get out of the storm. He caught sight of a cave high above the canyon, so he flew towards it. His landing wasn't as graceful as a bird's, but he touched down safely nonetheless. The storm was building, so the young dragon had to take shelter as soon as possible.

The weather was also getting worse for Richard and Chester, who was whinnying anxiously. They had just reached the edge of the forest. Richard knew that high winds combined with thunder and lightning in a forest were not a good mix.

"Easy, Chester," said Richard, trying to calm his friend down. "We'll find Bear Castle soon enough; we just need to find the right direction." But the minute they stepped into the forest, Richard became disorientated and very unsure. He knew they were starting to get lost. "Do you know where we're going, bud?" he asked Chester. "Because I don't."

The chestnut stallion shook his head. Suddenly, they heard a low, daunting growl. Chester's ears flicked from one direction to another, trying to detect the danger that might be out there. Out of the shadows burst a wolf. Just as the beast was closing in, Richard yelled, "Go, Chester, YAAAA!" Chester took off like an arrow, carrying his master away.

Chester galloped, while the wolf followed, letting out a blood-chilling howl. Then to make things worse, Richard and Chester realised that, where there's one wolf, there's usually a pack. In no time at all, the pack had the pair completely surrounded. For the first time in their lives, the friends were in real danger. Richard reached for his father's sword and leaped to the ground. "Chester, I need you to watch my back," he said. Chester nodded, ready to kick out at any danger around them.

One of the wolves stared at Richard holding the sword; his eyes glared, and his mouth watered. The pack lunged as one, Richard barrel-rolled, blocked and slashed three of the pack. Then two wolves charged at Chester, who reared up and stomped on their backs, immobilising them. Then he kicked two more of the pack who were attacking from behind. But even with the boy and the horse working together, it was going to be difficult to keep the pack at bay.

Suddenly, a flaming arrow swooped out of nowhere and struck the pack leader, wounding him. Richard and Chester were surprised. "Did you see that, bud?" Richard called to his friend. Chester shrugged his shoulders, then, swiftly, a shadowy figure in a hooded cloak appeared out of the darkness.

The figure stood between the two friends and the pack. With a sprinkling of combustible dust and a volley of flaming arrows, it sent the wolves packing, back into the forest. At first, Richard was thankful to the stranger for saving his life, but he was also cautious.

"Who are you?" he asked. The figure looked at him, then at Chester and then ran off into the forest. Richard called out.

"Wait, wait a minute, I didn't catch your name." He tried to run after the figure, but Chester caught his coat.

"Wiiiihihi," he whinnied.

"Come on, Chester, don't you want to find out the name of the person who just saved our lives?" Richard asked. But the equine shook his head. The horse didn't want his master getting mixed up with the wrong crowd. But Richard wouldn't take no for an answer and took off in the direction of the figure.

It's tough being friends with a human, Chester thought, but, remembering his promise to Bonnie, he followed.

Richard searched the forest, but there was no sign of the shadowy figure. "Are you playing hide and seek with me? I play that game with my horse all the time," he called. "I mean no harm and I just want to thank you for saving us." They searched until they came across a large tree with a hole in it.

"Hey, Chester," Richard called. "We'll rest here for the night and then continue to the castle in the morning." Just as they were about to settle down, an arrow came out of nowhere and behind them again was the cloaked figure.

"Who are you?" it asked. Richard drew his sword, but immediately another arrow knocked it out of his hands. Chester stepped between Richard and the figure, snorting and pawing the ground aggressively. The figure asked, "Now, I'll ask again, who are you?"

"Who am I?" asked Richard. "I was about to ask you the same thing."

The figure aimed its bow and arrow at Richard's shoulder. "If you won't give me an answer," it threatened, "this arrow's going straight into your shoulder."

Richard was growing angry, but that was also the reason why Chester was here, to help him realise that violence wasn't always the way out. So, Chester whinnied loudly and stared directly into Richard's eyes. Richard took some deep breaths, calmed himself, paused and then finally said, "My name is Richard Rosemary, and I don't want any trouble."

"Did my father send you?" the figure asked again. Richard was confused.

"Er, no. First of all, I don't even know who your father is..." The figure let the arrow loose, but instead of hitting Richard in the shoulder, it hit the tree stump he was standing in front of. Richard realised what a good shot the figure was.

"You'd better not be lying, or you know where the next one is going," it threatened.

"Okay, okay," Richard reassured. "Look, we are just passing through the forest to find Bear Castle because my ambition is to become a knight to the King of Bear." Richard explained that he and Chester were looking for a place to spend the night and escape the storm. The figure felt like this young man was telling the truth, so it lowered its bow and arrow.

"Follow me," it said reluctantly. "You'll catch your death."

Richard and Chester looked at each other, shrugged their shoulders and followed.

At Havoc Creek, Wisdom was about to have his own surprise. The cave echoed with eerie sounds of water dripping from the ceiling. Suddenly, a shady snarl sounded. Wisdom opened his eyes to find another dragon in a threatening position. "What are you doing in my cave?" she snarled.

Wisdom was afraid and didn't know how to react. "Well, you see..." he stuttered anxiously. Before he had finished speaking, the female dragon fired ice from her mouth; instinctively and rapidly, Wisdom unfurled his wings, as a shield. He was just about to explain why he was there, when the female whistle-breath charged and knocked him over onto his back. As she pinned him down, Wisdom's curved horns started to glow.

"Please," said Wisdom, "I don't want any trouble, I'm just looking for answers..."

Suddenly, recognising the glow on his horns, the female dragon stepped off him. "Drakon?" she asked in surprise. "Can it be?"

Wisdom was becoming very confused. "What? Huh? Who? Who is Drakon? My name is Wisdom."

The female dragon approached slowly and said gently, "I don't blame you for not remembering; after all, you were only an egg. Whistle-breaths share, with some shorebirds and crocodilians, the ability to cheep inside the egg and a mother never forgets a voice." Wisdom was surprised. Could this be his long-lost real mother or was this a trick? "I guess, by the expression on your face, you have some questions."

Wisdom nodded. His mother paused and allowed him to begin. "First of all, who am I? Where do I come from? What am I really? How come I have strange abilities? And are you my real mother?" he asked.

"Yes," she replied, "and I have so much to tell you."

She led Wisdom to a remote corner of the cave. The dragon mother let out a soft grunt and glow-worms lit up the cave. She said, "Drakon was the name that I gave you when you were an egg. It was my job to protect you and your brothers and sisters…"

"I have brothers and sisters?" Wisdom interrupted.

"Shhh…" soothed his mother. Wisdom obeyed, quietening down, wanting to know more. She continued. "You and your siblings were laid in this cave, far away from man, for very good reason.

"Centuries ago, we dragons were free to roam Muddle Worth across the wetlands, plains and mountains, even to the high seas. You and I are part of a species called whistle-breaths or fish-eaters. We used to travel to the lake to hunt for our meals and rest on the peninsula. Our ancestors happily shared the fishing grounds with the bears and other creatures, as there was plenty for us all. We were settled and happy in our homeland and had the land to ourselves, until man came."

Wisdom listened intently. His mother explained that man had always respected but also feared dragons and bears. When humans moved deeper into Muddle Worth a hundred years ago, they had divided the land into the four kingdoms. They then drove the dragons and bears away from the lake and built a castle on the peninsula.

"But why do men fear us?" Wisdom asked.

"Because, my boy, humans fear what they don't understand. Our ancestors found other fishing grounds in the remote wetlands. We dragons happily shared those with other creatures, large and small, until the volcano erupted five years ago, causing the wetlands to start drying out. Our paradise is now nothing but a barren wasteland. So, we have been forced to try to find food back at the lake and beyond the borders of Muddle Worth and have come back into conflict with man."

She went on to explain that she had had to steal fish from a human fishing fleet to feed herself and to nourish Wisdom and his siblings, but that, just as her eggs were about to hatch, a gang of men had found her, destroyed her nest and some of her eggs and scattered the others. She said she had no idea how many, if any, of her eggs had survived.

She also said that she thought that she would never see her children again. Her story continued as she told Wisdom about the young human who had saved her from being held captive in the castle. Suddenly, she stopped and looked at Wisdom, her eyes soft and full of love. "I cannot believe you're alive, my little Drakon, all grown up," she said.

Wisdom was fascinated and very keen to understand how he'd got his abilities. "How did I get these powers?" he asked. But even his mother wasn't ready to explain. All she wanted was to spend time with the son she thought she had lost for ever.

CHAPTER 14

Unexpected Journeys

Richard and Chester followed the shadowy figure deep into the large tree and then into an underground lair. As soon as they arrived, the figure took the cloak off and revealed itself. It was Maranda still in hiding.

"So, you're a woman?" asked Richard, surprised.

Maranda turned. "You've got a problem with that?" she asked sharply.

Richard didn't want to offend her, so he said, "Nope. I guess anyone can be a warrior these days."

Maranda scowled at him. Her time alone had made her wary and her autism was making her defensive.

The three of them settled around a campfire, in an uneasy silence. Eventually, Richard said, "So, I told you my name, what's yours?"

"Does it really matter?" Maranda asked, feeling in a dip.

Richard realised that Maranda might be feeling anxious. He often felt the same with strangers, so tried hard not to put her under more pressure. "Look," began Richard, gently smiling at Maranda. "You just saved our lives. Chester and I are really grateful. I find it's better if I get to know the kind of people I meet along the way, so please tell me your name whenever you're ready."

Maranda found it difficult to compete with Richard's

persistence, so she took a deep breath and answered. "Okay. Maranda… that's my name."

Richard looked at Chester, who was encouraging him to talk some more. Taking his courage in his hands, he said, "So, pleased to meet you, Maranda, we're kind of lost."

"You don't say," she replied sarcastically.

"Anyway, we're looking for Bear Castle. You wouldn't happen to know how to get there, would you?" Richard asked.

"Don't know, don't care," Maranda retorted.

Richard looked at her, feeling concerned and sensing that she had a story to tell. "Um, have you always been this cranky? No, no, don't tell me, let me guess, a lovers' tiff?"

"No."

"Lost in archery class?"

"No."

"A family spat?"

"Maybe."

"Oh, I get it, your family said something to offend you and you ran away."

Maranda lost patience. "LOOK, Richard Rosemary," she snapped, "I am tired, alone and I am trying to learn how to survive. What I need right now is peace and quiet. One more word out of you and I will leave you to the wolves, understand?"

Richard, recognising that more talking would achieve nothing, nodded his head.

"Good, now go to sleep," Maranda said, as she stepped away from him.

Chester snorted after her. "Pppppphhhh!" and turned to his master.

"You know, buddy, my gut says that, although her anxiety is making her one moody girl, she knows more than she is letting on. I think we should give her time and try to get on her good side, if we're going to find our way to…"

"GO TO SLEEP!" came Maranda's voice from across the lair.

"All right, no need to yell, I'm going, good night."

And they all went to sleep.

In the morning, Richard was outside the old tree, practising his sword play, while Chester was admiring the sights and sounds of nature and browsing on a berry bush. Maranda felt bad for what she had said, so she went out into the forest to forage items for breakfast: birds' eggs, mushrooms, berries and bugs for protein. But she took care only to take as much as they needed from the forest. After a lengthy sword practice, Richard realised he could smell fried eggs and mushrooms. He turned around to find Maranda preparing breakfast.

"Morning," he said.

"Morning," she said in return. "I hope you like eggs."

"My father used to make me collect eggs for breakfast on the farm," Richard said.

For the first time, Maranda smiled. "Listen, I want to apologise for my behaviour last night."

Richard was torn between the fact that a strange girl had wanted nothing to do with him the previous evening and the

fact that she was now trying to be kind. He decided to give her the benefit of the doubt.

They sat around the fire and Maranda shared out the eggs.

"Shall we start over?" Maranda asked. Richard looked at Chester for support and his friend gave him a nudge of encouragement.

"Okay, my name is Richard," he said. "Richard Rosemary, son of Samuel and Bonnie Rosemary. This is Chester, my horse."

"Nice name. I'm Maranda of Bear," she replied. After they had finished eating, they took a walk through the forest, talking about themselves and their families.

"My father was a knight, who fought bravely for what he stood for, protecting the innocent," Richard said. "I don't really understand why, but my father then gave it up to be a farmer, but he is the reason why I want to become a knight. I want to defend Muddle Worth and make a difference in life."

"That's great," said Maranda, trying to sound cheerful, but feeling very anxious because of the way knights treated creatures like dragons.

"Well, I've explained about my father, what about yours? What does he do for a living?" asked Richard.

Maranda felt very unsure. She was afraid what would happen if Richard found out that she was the daughter of the King of Bear. "Well, um, he was a warrior, but then he got transferred to the post of a castle guard," she said, covering her tracks. "He was one of the knights who went to Havoc Creek to capture a dragon and destroy her eggs."

Suddenly, they heard a loud crackling sound and found themselves caught up in a huge net. While they were struggling to free themselves, out of the bushes came a large goblin and a bald dwarf.

"Well, looks like we're going to eat fine today, Flynn," said the dwarf, licking his ugly lips.

"You do realise you're going to lose your heads when we get out?!" Richard warned.

Instead, the goblin and dwarf laughed, not taking Richard's threats seriously.

"If you're going to warn or threaten someone, try to pick a moment when you're not caught in a huge net," whispered Maranda, sarcastically.

"Thanks, I'll remember that next time," Richard retorted, under his breath.

Their capture didn't go unnoticed. Chester was alerted by the cries and wanted to free his master and the girl, but knew he couldn't do it alone.

"Hey," he called to a bluejay. "I need you to ask Synder to take this message to a friend of mine called Wisdom," he whispered in the bird's ear, who flew off quickly to find Synder.

CHAPTER 15

Friends Unite

At Havoc Creek, Wisdom was enjoying spending time with his mother. He was also learning how to control his dragon abilities and to use them in the right way.

"This is awesome," cried Wisdom in excitement. His mother was glad to see her long-lost son feeling happy. Just then, she spotted an injured bat, who had fallen from the cave ceiling.

"Son," she said, "this bat is injured, let's have it for lunch." But Wisdom knew he couldn't let an innocent creature suffer, so he picked it up. As he did so, his dragon scales and curved horns started to glow.

As he glowed, the cave walls shone with a myriad of spectacular colour and light. His mother smiled, realising that he had inherited the healing powers given to one whistle-breath in every clutch. The bat started to stir, gently flapped its wings, then, a moment later, took off into the depths of the cave.

"You know, Drakon," she said. "You have a heart of light, the magic inherited ability to heal the sick and wounded and, I believe, the soul of a dragon who can unite lands together." Wisdom was amazed and felt delighted that he was making both mothers proud.

Just then, Synder flew rapidly into the cave, landed on Wisdom's nose and said urgently, "Wisdom, I bring a message from your friend, Chester the horse. His master and a brown-haired girl have been captured by a goblin and a dwarf and they need your help."

Wisdom looked out of the cave to the wide lands beyond and then back to his mother. "I have to go, a friend of mine needs me," he said softly.

The mother dragon took a deep breath and said, "Be careful, my baby." Then she hugged him.

"I will, Mum, and I hope to make you proud." He took off and flew out high across the land to find his best friend.

Meanwhile, Chester was silently following the goblin and dwarf to a cottage deep in the forest. They had lived in this cottage for as long as anyone could remember.

"I'll get the fire going," said Dug, the dwarf.

"I'll get the table laid and prepare our food," said Flynn, the goblin. No sooner had he turned his back than Richard and Maranda had broken their way out of the net, grabbed their weapons and sprang into action. Finally, after a frantic tussle, when Richard and Maranda worked together, using all the skills they had perfected during many hours of practice, the farm boy and the princess had the goblin and dwarf pinned.

"Nice moves, Maranda!" said Richard, winking at her. "Don't say I didn't warn you, beast," he said, pointing his sword at Flynn.

"Please," Flynn begged. "We only wanted something to eat, that's all."

"And how does that include us?" asked Maranda sternly, demanding an explanation.

"Well, you see, lassie," began Dug, "me and my accomplice used to have plenty of food in our cottage, but then a wicked sorceress, named Velha, sent her brother, Dagger, with his mob and they took everything." Suddenly he realised he'd heard Richard saying the girl's name and bowed. "Surely you can understand pain and hunger and what it drives creatures to, Your Highness?"

Maranda lowered her bow and told Richard to lower his sword. Then Flynn bowed. Richard was confused.

"Your Highness? What are you talking about?" he asked.

"She didn't tell you, lad?" Dug said, looking from one to the other. "Yeah, she's Maranda, Princess of Bear."

Richard looked at Maranda in surprise. "Is this true?" he asked her. Maranda was scared; she didn't know what to say, but she knew there was no point in denying it, so she nodded. Richard began to bow.

"Stand up, please," Maranda demanded; she wanted him to see her as more than royalty. Richard stood up, shook his head (suddenly there was a lot to take in) and left without another word. Maranda felt awful for leading Richard on like a fool.

"Give the young lad time, Your Highness," said Dug, "he'll come around."

Richard sat outside the cottage on a fallen log, feeling

totally foolish. *I can't believe she's a princess,* he said to himself. *She saves my life and now she treats me like a fool.* Just as he was feeling sorry for himself, he heard a rustle in the bushes. He grabbed his sword, preparing for anything. Then, out of the bushes stepped Chester, who had been watching them from afar.

"Chester, am I ever glad to see you, bud."

"Neigh!" Chester licked his face with joy and then Richard told him that their friend Maranda was the Princess of Bear.

"And she didn't even tell me," he said. "You know what, boy, we're better off without her, let's go."

As Richard started to mount Chester, Maranda stopped him. "Please wait," she said. "Look, I'm sorry, I guess I should have told you that I am a princess. I was just scared that, if you found out who I was, you would've reported me to my father."

Richard gave her a sad, hurt look and then said, "Keep talking. Why did you run away?"

Maranda took a deep breath and replied, "I ran away because of what my father had done. When I was young, a group of fishermen came running into our family's throne room and told my parents that a dragon had attacked their fishing fleet. I didn't believe it because I believe that dragons are more than simple beasts people fear and despise and that, if the dragon had attacked the fleet, it would have been for good reason. Before I could say anything, my father, the king, told his loyal knights to find the dragon and bring it to our castle. The knights captured her and then my father locked her away in the dungeon. I was devastated, not only because of the injustice to the dragon, but also because they wanted me to agree to be engaged to some prince from the Kingdom of Dragon to appease the King of Dragon, so I refused." She explained to Richard how she'd freed the female dragon from the dungeons and that she had recently heard from the forest spirits that the King of Dragon had threatened war against the Kingdom of Bear if the dragon was harmed.

Then she told Richard that he and Chester were the first real friends she'd ever had. Great tears of regret ran down her cheeks. Richard felt conflicted. He still wanted to find his own way to Bear Castle, but he also wanted to stay and be a good friend to the princess, who had clearly been through so much and now needed some comfort. So, he chose to get off his horse and enveloped her in a hug. "My autism has always made it hard for me to make friends and I'd never had any friends until Chester was born. Now I would like to be your friend. Thank you for being honest with me."

Touched, Maranda embraced Richard in return. She was secretly pleased to have a new friend, who also had autism. But she wanted time to process this unexpected news, before finding the right time to tell Richard that she was autistic too. Chester was delighted because his boy looked so happy to have another friend. Suddenly, he heard marching feet and alarm cries from the woodland creatures. The smell of black magic filled the air. "Neeeeeeigh!" He whinnied in fear.

"Woah, woah, bud," said Richard, trying to calm his friend down. "What is it?"

Chester turned his head towards the sound of loud yelling and marching feet coming from the west.

Maranda said, "We must find Dug and Flynn and hide." They hurried into the cottage to warn the goblin and the dwarf.

"An angry mob is coming," said Maranda. "We have to move."

Flynn looked through the window to see a mob led by a military-looking figure, with a fishhook through his nose. "It's Dagger," he cried.

"Quick," said Dug, turning to Richard, Maranda and Chester. "Go out the back way and get as far away from here as you can. We'll take care of things here."

BANG, BANG went the door.

"All right, dwarf, open this door or WE WILL KICK IT DOWN!" bellowed Dagger.

Dug opened the door and said, "Look, Dagger, we haven't got anything for you, we're all out, remember?"

"Don't patronise me, half pint," spat Dagger. "I know you're hiding something, and my sister wants it. Search the place," he commanded the mob, who then pushed roughly past Dug and Flynn and into the cottage.

Out on the edge of the forest, Chester took Richard and Maranda as far as his strong legs could carry him. "Woah, woah, boy," Richard called, stopping him.

"Why are you stopping?" asked Maranda crossly.

"Flynn and Dug can't handle an angry mob by themselves and we can't leave them," Richard retorted.

"In case you haven't noticed, there are only three of us and we're short of reinforcements," Maranda snapped back. But, before the two could start arguing, Chester noticed something approaching in the sky.

It was Wisdom. Chester whinnied with excitement to attract his friend's attention.

"Oh great, just what we need, a dragon," said Richard, sounding anxious.

"Wait, wait," said Maranda, who was looking closely at Wisdom as he landed, thinking that he looked just like the female whistle-breath she had freed from the dungeon.

Chester was relieved to see his friend. "How has it been?" he asked Wisdom. "Did you find what you were looking for?"

Wisdom hurriedly told Chester about his long-lost mother, about the cave where he was laid and his birth name. "And above all that, I have discovered I have abilities I never knew I had," he said.

"You mean, besides breathing ice?" Chester asked. Wisdom nodded.

"Look," said Maranda, stepping in and winking at Richard. "I hate to break up the bromance, but we've got a war to stop, after we save Flynn and Dug."

Richard smiled and said, "My dad always told me that a true knight's role is to help those in need, and that's what I'm going to do. Who's with me?" Everyone nodded and huddled.

It was time to discuss a plan.

CHAPTER 16

The Defenders

Back in the forest, Dagger had taken Dug and Flynn hostage and was burning the cottage to ashes.

"Velha would like a word with you, boys," he growled. Dug and Flynn were bruised and battered from Dagger's attack.

The mob stepped aside to reveal a pale-faced sorceress. Her left hand went up to cast a spell. "I took you two scroungers in out of the goodness of my heart, and this is how you thank me?" she snarled.

Flynn tried to explain. "Look, we just haven't got any more money or food..."

"SILENCE!" The sorceress hissed in anger. Suddenly, from the bushes and the trees, something picked off each member of the dark mob. Some were dragged into the bushes and some hit by arrows.

"You know the penalty for non-payment," said Velha. "I did warn you, but my warnings fell on deaf ears. Dagger, finish them off!"

Dagger was about to strike the dwarf with his blade, when a sword blocked him. It was Richard. "If there's one thing I hate in this world, it's bullies!" he snapped.

"Get out of the way, boy, before you get hurt," Dagger snarled. But Richard wasn't going anywhere.

An arrow flew at Velha's head, until she deflected it with

a spell. “I wasn't expecting guests so soon,” she cackled, with an evil smile.

Out of nowhere, Maranda appeared with bow and arrows at the ready.

“You're done hurting innocent people,” she said.

Velha chuckled. “Innocent? Ha, if only you knew what their lives were like. My dear child, I took them out of the wild, gave them a life and now I own their sorry backsides.”

Maranda had had enough. “Over my dead body,” she said, firing three arrows rapidly at Velha.

The pale-faced sorceress caught two, but the third cut her deep across the right cheek. “So be it!” she screamed angrily. She cast another spell and tree roots wrapped around the princess from arm to foot.

“Someone should've taught you respect. To make sure you get the message, watch your handsome man suffer.” Velha commanded her brother and the mob to attack Richard from all sides. Suddenly, Velha was encased in ice. Wisdom and Chester sprang out of the bushes too. The battle was on.

Dagger shouted to his diminishing mob, who attacked again. Richard blocked, slashed and freed Maranda from the tree roots. Chester bucked and kicked, Maranda slashed and shot many arrows and Wisdom spat ice shards, head butted and tail swished. Richard leaped on Chester and Maranda climbed onto Wisdom's back. The friends worked together and brought the mob to its knees, begging for mercy.

Dagger did not take kindly to defeat. “I won't be beaten by kids and THEIR PETS!” he roared. He charged, readying to run his sword into Wisdom, but Richard jumped in front of him, blocking the attack. “You just don't know when to quit,” Dagger snarled.

“On guard, bully,” shouted Richard and a sword duel began. Richard pictured Dagger as the bully he had stood up to in Roland Town, but he had learned from that experience to keep his temper. The others could only watch the duel play out, but they stood ready, in case their friend needed help.

Finally, Dagger knocked Richard to his knees. "Any last words, boy?" he asked, raising his sword.

"Yes, heads up!" cried Richard, as Maranda fired one of her arrows right at Dagger's head and a tail swish from Wisdom knocked him flying. The friends cheered and Flynn and Dug joined in, hardly able to believe that Velha and Dagger were defeated.

"We owe you and your friends our lives, Princess," Flynn said gratefully.

"Aye, lassie, we are forever in your debt," added Dug.

"We're only too pleased to help," Richard said. "After all, we are a team, and we have each other's backs."

Wisdom turned to Chester and said, "I can't believe we stood up to a dark mob; awesome, right?"

"I couldn't agree more, my friend," Chester replied, and the two of them high-fived.

But there was no time to celebrate. Maranda knew that the war could commence at any time. "Guys, we have to get back to the castle," she said. "My father could be preparing for war."

"If you need any help, send for us," replied Dug, then Richard mounted Chester, Maranda climbed onto Wisdom and, after saying farewell to Flynn and Dug, they rode and flew off out of the forest as fast as they could towards Bear Castle.

In their hurry to move on, they had not realised that Velha had melted her way out of the ice and had escaped with her brother's dead body. Flynn and Dug knew they would have to be ready in case they were needed. They looked sadly at their burnt-out cottage, then set about clearing up the devastation around their forest home.

Seeing the kids take off, the pale-faced sorceress burned with revenge.

CHAPTER 17

You're All Better Than This

Back at Bear Castle, King Thomas was in his throne room feeling bad about what had become of his daughter. Suddenly, Jasper, the captain of the Bear Kingdom knights, came into the throne room and said, "Your Majesty, we've received word from the King of Dragon that he's on his way here now. What do you want to do?"

The king took a deep breath, rose from the throne and said, "Captain, ready the army, we must defend Bear Kingdom at all costs."

The knights put their armour on, sharpened their swords and readied their shields. The people were shepherded inside the castle for safety, along with their children. After kissing his queen, the king mounted his horse and started to lead his army out onto the battlefield on the lake's shore to confront the Dragon Kingdom's army.

The army appeared on the horizon.

"I must have a word with their king, before any action is taken." King Thomas told Jasper to request an audience with the King of Dragon. Everyone heard him and lowered their arms to signal to the Dragon Kingdom army that the kings should speak. The King of Dragon, Huang, approached slowly, accompanied by his knight commander. Huang and Thomas exchanged stern looks.

"Thomas!" said Huang.

"Huang!" said Thomas in return.

"Where is the dragon?"

"We no longer have it; it escaped from my castle dungeon. My knights have been out searching, to return it to you or set it free, as you command. You and I can end this here and now before any blood is shed."

"If what you say is true, then I would consider sparing you and your kingdom. If you're lying to me, there will be consequences," King Huang replied, staring at King Thomas.

The two kings exchanged a final glance and then returned to their own armies, neither willing to trust the other. Jasper asked King Thomas, "Do they want to fight or retreat, Sire?"

King Thomas looked seriously at his army and started to speak. "Brothers of Bear," he said. "Today I stand before you, as not just your king, but as a warrior. I have tried to negotiate with King Huang, but now that we no longer have the dragon, I fear they will attack us. So, we must do whatever we can to protect our kingdom and our people."

On the other side of the field, King Huang also spoke to his army. "My brothers of Dragon, King Thomas of Bear claims the creature has escaped, but I do not believe him. So, we'll show them the consequences of lying and holding our precious whistle-breath hostage."

Although neither army wanted war, their kings' pride and suspicion was too great. A cry went up from both kings, "No matter how this ends, IT ENDS TODAY!"

The queen and the people of Bear stood within the castle walls and looked on as the armies readied for battle.

"Be safe, my love," Queen Jules said softly, with tears streaming down her face.

The knights locked eyes with their opponents and tightened their grip on their weapons. King Huang raised his blade, then signalled to the archers.

"Archers, FIRE!" ordered the commander. Flaming arrows came falling out of the sky. The Bear army raised their shields, deflecting the arrows. Unfortunately, it was only the first wave.

King Thomas and King Huang raised their swords, pointed them forward and yelled, "CHARGE!" A terrible battle began to shake the land.

Without warning, a dragon's shrill cry caused the fighting to stop. The armies stared in the direction of the sound. With a flapping of his mighty wings, down came Wisdom with Princess Maranda on his back.

"Everybody, stop!" she cried and then, with a galloping of hooves, Chester arrived, with Richard on his back.

"Daughter, what is the meaning of this? Step aside," Thomas ordered.

But Maranda wouldn't move. "No, father, you need to hear the truth." She looked backwards and forwards between the two armies.

"All of you," she called, "my name is Princess Maranda of Bear. I have come to tell you the truth. The female dragon is not dead or in the dungeon. She is out there and free; how? Because I set her free. I don't like it when any creatures of our beloved Muddle Worth are harmed and mistreated. Today, I stand before you with this incredible creature. This is the offspring of the whistle-breath dragon, who stole fish from our fishing fleet out of hunger and desperation. Look at yourselves fighting each other for petty reasons. We shouldn't be inflicting harm on each other or on other living creatures, who share our land. We're not that different from them and we're better than this. We should invite the dragons, bears and other creatures back to feed in the lake, to restore the balance destroyed when our ancestors drove them from their ancient fishing grounds. Our kingdoms have been at peace for too many years for us to start fighting now. We should not be fighting. We have so much more to gain by continuing to work together to protect Muddle Worth from the dangers beyond all our borders."

Both the armies and the people of Bear were won over by the princess' words.

"She really works a crowd, doesn't she?" Richard whispered to Chester.

As Maranda was speaking, light blazed through the sky and shone over Maranda and Wisdom. Kings Thomas and Huang felt very bad about allowing their kingdoms to reach the point of war.

Thomas approached his daughter and said, "Maranda,

I'm sorry for everything, I should've been a better father and a better king."

Maranda felt sorry for her father, so she dismounted Wisdom and approached the king. "I'm sorry I ran away, and I hope in future to be the daughter you deserve."

Father and daughter embraced. King Thomas threw down his sword and ordered his knights to stand down. He approached King Huang to discuss a peaceful solution. "Huang, I'm sorry for the misunderstanding; it turns out my daughter is as smart as her mother," he said.

"I suppose we can negotiate." Huang smiled, feeling very relieved.

Both armies returned to their kingdoms. As Richard and Chester approached Bear Castle, Richard said to Maranda, "So, this is Bear Castle."

"Yeah, it may not look much, but it's home." The other knights were a bit suspicious of Richard's arrival, until Maranda told them that he was with her. "Richard, would you like to meet my family?" she asked.

To begin with, Richard was nervous. It's not every day you get to meet the royal family of Bear! "All right," he said. "I'm just unsure what they will think of me because I'm a farm boy and you're a princess…"

"Look, you let me worry about my parents," Maranda reassured him. "Just follow my lead and speak when you are spoken to. Everything is going to be fine."

When they reached the castle, they left Chester and Wisdom outside.

"Well," said Chester to Wisdom. "We just took on an evil sorceress and prevented a war from getting out of hand."

"Yeah," replied Wisdom. "I say we had a pretty great day and we've certainly watched each other's tails like we promised. I just wish that Tonto could have been with us to experience this for himself."

While the two animals were chatting outside, the farm boy and the princess went through into the great halls of the castle. They entered the throne room and approached the king and queen.

"My baby, I thought we'd lost you," Queen Jules said, hugging her daughter and beaming.

"Thank you, Mum. I've missed you," said Maranda.

"And just who might you be, young man?" asked King Thomas, approaching Richard. Richard took a bow, to show his respect, as he greeted the king and queen.

"Mum, Dad, I'd like you to meet my friend, Richard Rosemary," said Maranda.

"It is an honour to meet you, Your Majesties," said Richard.

"Did you help our daughter back home?" asked the queen.

Richard was stuck for the moment until… "Well, ma'am, as it turns out, we helped each other. Your daughter saved my life while I was on my way to Bear Castle."

"You're Samuel Rosemary's son?" King Thomas asked, trying to piece the puzzle together.

"Yes!" exclaimed Richard. "He is my father, Your Majesty. All I've ever wanted to do is to make a difference. My father told me that he used to be a knight, a defender of the helpless. I also like horses, hate bullies and my dearest ambition is to be a knight like him. Even if it takes a long time, I'll do anything to achieve my goal."

CHAPTER 18

A New Lease on Life

Richard was getting acquainted with King Thomas. They were exploring the castle inside and out, taking in the grounds, the great halls, the kitchen and the dining rooms.

"Your father and I go way back," explained Thomas. "He and I trained to be knights in the Wolf Kingdom. My father wanted me to train under cover away from Bear Kingdom without the pressure of everyone knowing I was the heir to the Bear throne. He arranged for your father to come with me, as we were friends at school. While training together to become knights, we became the best of friends."

"Funny, Dad never mentioned anything about you, Your Majesty," said Richard.

"The truth is," said Thomas, "that my father and the King of Wolf swore us to secrecy. They feared that our fellow knights might not be happy training with a prince."

Thomas continued on, describing his comradeship with Samuel, how they'd had each other's backs on the field of battle and how their friendship had developed, until the day Thomas' father passed away, making him the King of Bear. At first, Samuel served as one of Thomas' most loyal knights back in Bear. But then Samuel asked Thomas if he could be released from his service as a knight to marry his love and settle down on a farm. Thomas rewarded Samuel for his loyal service by granting him Rosemary Farm.

Richard told King Thomas that Samuel had taught him to work hard, do his best and be true to himself. He also told him that Samuel had trained him in the basics of being a knight and about his best friend, Chester, his horse.

Queen Jules liked Richard and wanted to be hospitable to him. She suggested that Richard should be their guest for dinner.

"Your Majesty, I would be honoured to have dinner with you," he replied graciously. Princess Maranda was happy to have a friend of hers for dinner with her family. In the evening, the family and Richard gathered around the table.

"So, Maranda, sweetie," began Jules, "tell us about where you met Richard."

At first, the princess was unsure about telling her family, but she took a deep breath and spoke. "Well, Mum, Dad, I met Richard and his friend Chester in the forest. He was on his way to our castle because he wants to become one of our knights," she said.

Now it was Richard's turn. "Permission to speak, Your Majesty," he said politely.

The king admired the boy's manners, so he said, "Permission granted."

Richard continued. "The reason why I want to be a knight is that, for as long as I can remember, other kids have picked on me. I want to use my power to focus and work hard to show others that I can make a difference. I want to dedicate myself to learning how to defend myself and fight for Muddle Worth and my family." He also told the king that, if he didn't fight for his family's farm, they could lose it.

While Richard was telling the royal family about Rosemary Farm, in the castle stables, Chester and Wisdom were resting and discussing what would happen next.

"Listen, Chest," said the dragon, "I can't stay in the kingdom for much longer, there may be more of my siblings out there. I have to find out what has happened to them."

Chester was a little surprised. "Oh, so where will you go?" he asked. "I mean, we just got back together."

"You see, old chap, your friend is right," a voice said, as a light grey stallion in the stall next door to Chester cut into the conversation.

"What shall I call you?" asked Chester.

"They call me Lance," the grey stallion replied.

"My name is Chester, and this is Wisdom," the chestnut stallion said.

"Pleased to meet you," replied Lance. "You see, lad, freedom is the right of all creatures large and small, man and beast. There'll come a moment when young Wisdom will have to find his own way in the world, make his own mistakes and hopefully learn from them."

The king told Maranda to show her new friend to his room for the night.

"I have to say, Maranda," said Richard, "I was really anxious meeting your parents. Hope I haven't embarrassed you so far."

"Oh no, Richard, I believe you acted with the greatest courtesy, I'm proud of you."

When they reached the spare room in the third tower, Maranda said, "Well, what do you think?"

Richard took a look around the luxurious room from top to bottom. "It looks excellent," he said. "Thank you, Maranda, for all your hospitality. If only my parents could see me now!"

"I'm only too pleased to help a friend," Maranda said, feeling like she had done a good job.

"Well, good night and see you tomorrow."

In the morning, Richard had his breakfast with the royal family. King Thomas was very thoughtful for a long time and then suggested that the kingdom set Wisdom free.

"I was thinking the same thing, Dad, but, it is a shame, as I am just getting acquainted with him!" said Maranda.

"You know that the dragon is not a pet, and he has to roam free," The king said seriously. Even the queen agreed on this one.

"What do you say, Richard?" asked Maranda.

"I say that no animal big or small should be locked up and we should let Wisdom go if he wants to."

Outside the castle walls, the people and armies gathered to watch Wisdom be set free. The dragon looked out at the wide expanse of the valley and then back at his friends.

"I'm going to miss you, my friend," said Maranda. "Please take care of yourself. I hope you find what you're looking for out there." She kissed him on his forehead and, in return, Wisdom gave her a great big lick.

Then it was Richard's turn. "Well, we've had a great time together saving Muddle Worth from falling into a chaotic conflict. I hope we see you again soon," he said.

He let Chester have a moment with his friend.

"Ever since I found you in the river, I had a feeling life would change for us. You are the best friend I've ever had and I hate to see us separate..." Chester began.

But before he could finish, Wisdom cut in, "Hey, there's no place you can go that I won't be with you. If ever you need me, neigh as loud as you can."

Wisdom said farewell to his three best friends and then took off to search for his siblings and his place in the world. Chester pulled away from the people of Bear and galloped after Wisdom. He ran as fast and far as he could, until he came to the top of a high hill. He watched until Wisdom vanished over the forest and out of sight.

If you think this would be the last they would ever see of each other, think again! After all, remember, they promised that they would have each other's backs the whole way…!

About the Author

My name is Marcus Mason-Williams. I am an autistic artist, performer, storyteller and businessperson. Since I was young, I have loved drawing animals and telling stories. In 2021, I realised that I could turn my passions into a business, which is why I set up my own online business, CoolArt2021.co.uk, to sell my animal and nature inspired artwork and books. I both write and illustrate children's books. My first book was *Zooland, A Sign of Hope*. A copy was signed by the England football manager, Gareth Southgate, for use as a prize in a Special Olympics GB charity competition. *The Horse and the Dragon, Trials of Friendship* is my second book. I have achieved all this not despite my autism, but because of the strength and creativity it gives me. I hope that other people like me can see me and know that neurodivergent people can be successful and start our own businesses. Our autism is not a weakness, it is a strength that we just have to find ways to express!

Printed in Great Britain
by Amazon

49180364R00064